LINEAR TACTICAL SERIES

USA *TODAY* BESTSELLING AUTHOR
JANIE CROUCH

BLAZE: LINEAR TACTICAL

Chapter 1

"Black man sitting in the tree. Feeling like I've lost my damn mind . . ."

Kendrick Foster sang the words—to the tune of "Swing Low, Sweet Chariot"—while perched up in a giant ponderosa pine in the middle of the Wyoming wilderness.

He was actually half Black, other half Korean—both parts he claimed with equal pride—but including it all didn't fit the tune as well.

What would his Harvard or Yale colleagues say if they could see him now? This was definitely not where he'd envisioned himself ending up when he'd first started his cybersecurity studies.

His life had changed completely in the two years since he'd wandered into Oak Creek to help his boss at the time, Gabe Collingwood, get his sister back from some kidnappers.

And then somehow, he had never left.

It wasn't just the place that kept him here, although there was no doubt that this part of western Wyoming, complete with lush national forests and the picturesque Teton Mountains, was enough to enthrall even the most citified of them all. Which Kendrick didn't deny he was.

It was the people who'd convinced him to stay here—all without ever saying a word about it. Friends who had become family, anchoring him to a place he'd never thought he'd be.

Some of those same people were hunting him now—guns raised, ready to take him out of their equation, using whatever means they could. He needed to not forget that.

Friends who had turned enemies.

He studied the wilderness from his lookout for any sign of movement, humming the tune again under his breath.

"Dude, are you singing in a situation like this?" Dorian Lindstrom's voice echoed through Kendrick's head from the communication unit they were wearing.

The big man did not sound amused. Of course, he'd spent five weeks being tortured to within an inch of his life in an enemy prison camp a few years ago, so Dorian didn't find a lot of things amusing.

"You do know what's at stake here, right Blaze?" added Gavin.

Kendrick rolled his eyes. Gavin was another one who tended to take everything *life or death* seriously.

"Believe me, I'm well aware of what's at stake." Kendrick spoke low into his communication unit. "What we all have to lose if they defeat us."

"DEFCON one. That's what threat level this is," Baby chimed in.

Kendrick let out a sigh. "*Et tu, Brute*? I expected less Special Forces lingo from you, Baby, since you didn't drink the military Kool-Aid. We non-Rambo kids have to stick together."

"It just means this might possibly be the most dangerous mission any of us have ever been a part of," Gabe responded. He hadn't served in the Rangers with Dorian and Gavin but had been a Navy SEAL.

"More dangerous than when I sent you guys into that rescue attempt and we didn't have all the information and weren't sure about the level of danger and you almost got killed?"

"Which time?" four voices said in unison.

Kendrick made a face. Okay, there had been more than once when they'd had to trust each other with their lives. "Fair point."

"Stakes are higher this time, Blaze," Dorian said. His voice was the slightest bit uneven, which meant he was probably sprinting somewhere.

"Everything is on the line. We can't afford to lose." Gavin's voice was muffled. If he was where he was supposed to be, by now he was hidden far away from all of them, camouflaged by an area of overgrowth, deep into their enemy's territory.

Kendrick used his binoculars to look around the area again. "We've got no movement in the southwestern quadrant."

"Don't forget they know our weaknesses and aren't afraid to use them against us any way they can." Baby may not have the military experience of some of the others, but he was out here today, like Kendrick, to do whatever he could to make sure the good guys came out on top.

Because that's what the Linear men did—including those like Kendrick and Baby who weren't officially employed by the self-defense, weapons, and survival training company—when they were called upon. They showed up to help their friends fight their foes.

Even when it was DEFCON one. Especially when it was DEFCON one.

"We have to win this." Kendrick shifted the binoculars in the direction they figured the enemy would approach from. "Because I'm not drinking those fucking blue Electric

Smurfs again. And I'm definitely not doing that Cowboy Boogie."

Everybody groaned.

"You know they'll not only make us buy the drinks, they'll make us match them shot for shot if they win." Baby made a gagging sound.

"Then we make sure they don't win," Dorian countered. "Because I will never live down that dance."

It was sundown; time was running out.

"How many shots does everyone have left?" Gavin asked. "Everyone's still nearly full, right?"

"I'm down one from running into my sister earlier," Baby said. "Wavy was waiting to ambush me. Almost got me too."

Everyone else gave a report. They all still had full rounds in their guns.

Laser guns, that was.

It was boys versus girls in capture the flag. Losers had to buy drinks for the winning team tonight at the Eagle's Nest. And do the dance.

To make the game fair, anyone with prior military experience only had three shots available to them on their laser gun. For the guys that meant Dorian, Gavin, and Gabe. Baby and Kendrick had five.

On the girls' team, everyone but Ray had five shots. And Ray wasn't allowed to use a crossbow, since there was no such thing as a laser crossbow. But mostly because, if there had been such a thing, she would've already taken out the guys' entire team—she was that talented with the weapon.

The girls' team—the most dangerous enemy Kendrick and the guys had ever met—was made up of Dorian's wife Ray, Gavin's fiancée Lexi, Gabe's wife Jordan, Baby's sister Waverly . . .

And Neo. She was Kendrick's.

4

But damned if he knew *how* she was his. Some crazy mix between colleague and girlfriend. And enemy.

With Neo LeBarre, he never quite knew where he stood. For someone used to being the smartest person in the room . . . Kendrick liked the way she kept him on his toes. Confused him.

"Northeast quadrant is clear," Gabe reported in.

"It's way too quiet," Gavin muttered. "You see anything, Blaze?"

"Nothing. At all."

Which wasn't good.

Their strategy had been to make their flag relatively easily accessible, then pick the women off when they tried to get it. Play defensively, then get the girls' flag.

The women, after all, weren't known for their patience. They were all smart, strong, and cunning. They would bring the battle to the guys if the guys didn't take it to them.

Kendrick's phone buzzed in his pocket. He set it out on his leg so he could glance at the text but still keep a lookout all around him.

Looking forward to us drinking Electric Smurfs tonight. And seeing you dance.

Neo. It only took Kendrick two seconds to read the text, then his eyes were back out on the wilderness surrounding him.

I prefer whiskey, neat. You can buy me one when we win. And you can dance.

With him. But he wouldn't add that.

He typed without ever looking back at his phone. It was one of the advantages of how his brain worked. Glancing at a keyboard—any keyboard at any time—wasn't necessary.

There's going to be dancing tonight either way. I'm going to be wearing a dress. A strappy little number.

Oh shit.

5

He'd worked with Neo a half dozen times over the past few months, mostly to help the Linear Tactical team thwart whatever bad guy they were facing or get out of whatever danger they'd gotten themselves into.

He'd also seen her at a couple of the girls' nights out at the Eagle's Nest, a lot more loose and enjoying herself.

But he'd never seen her in a dress. He'd very much like to see those legs of hers in a strappy little dress.

"The girls are making their move, you guys." His voice came out a little hoarse over the comm unit.

"Did you see something?" Dorian asked. "How do you know?"

"I got a text from Neo about her wearing a strappy little dress tonight."

"Fuck, he's right," Baby said. "She's trying to distract him. I'm on my way."

"Me too." Gabe's voice was the slightest bit breathy. He was running.

"I just spotted two of them, I think Jordan and Wavy, coming around from the west," Gavin said. "I should be able to get them."

"I'm coming to you," Gabe said.

"Be care—" Kendrick trailed off at the next text.

Don't you want to see me in a dress? A short one? Cut down to . . .

Hell yes, he wanted to see her in a dress.

"Ghost, they have to know where I am," he said into the comm unit. "They can't get a good shot at me up here so Neo's trying to distract me."

And even knowing that, it was still working. Because the thought of sitting next to her at the bar later tonight, knowing he'd be able to reach out and touch the smooth skin of her leg underneath the skirt . . . It was triggering every fantasy he had.

"If she's texting you, it's keeping her busy too. Get down

while you can, so no one can ambush you," Dorian responded.

Kendrick started climbing down the rope ladder he and the guys had attached to the tree, sending a text partway.

How about when I win you save all your dances for me in your strappy little number.

The fact that he could take the ladder at such speed while texting, spoke to the changes in him in the months since he'd been in Oak Creek. He was never going to be at the level of awareness or fitness of these former Special Forces guys, but he could hold his own.

He was no longer the nerd who sat behind the computer.

And he dared say that nobody else could keep watch for enemy combatants, get down a tree, and text someone at the same time.

I think I'll be saving my dances for you either way. I've been thinking about you.

"The girls are definitely making their move." Kendrick's words were tight. There wasn't much he wanted more on this earth than to know Neoma LeBarre had been spending her time thinking about him.

But right now, he had to play the game, not let her get the upper hand. He shot back a text.

Oh yeah? Was I wearing naughty lingerie in your thoughts?

Kendrick ran back toward where they'd hidden their flag.

No. But maybe I wass.

Fuck. Neo was pulling out the big guns. But there were also two *s*'s on the word was. She was like him—moving fast while trying to type. She wouldn't make a mistake like that otherwise.

"I've got eyes on three of them." Kendrick couldn't tell exactly who'd said that. Gavin?

"Yeah, I see them." Baby. "Oh, sh—" There was a moment of silence. "I'm hit."

Baby was down. He wasn't allowed to say anything else.

"I got Wavy," Gavin said. "And I just saw—" Silence. "I'm down."

"I've got Neo in my sights," Gabe's voice was low. "She's moving down the southeast quadrant. I can take her out."

"I'm almost to you." Kendrick pushed himself faster. "She's up to something. We can flank her."

He spotted Neo up ahead, the much larger Gabe not far behind her. Gabe was about to take his shot when she made a sudden veer to the left.

"Shit," Gabe muttered. "I lost my shot."

"Don't worry, I've got her." Kendrick pushed faster so he could go wide, get around in front of her, and cut her off by some large boulders.

He still wanted to see her in a dress though. Would she still wear it even when she lost?

He came out around the other side of the boulder, gun raised.

Neo slid to a halt not twenty yards in front of him. She raised her hands, and he wondered if she was going to try to talk her way out of him shooting her.

But then she smiled.

"We had to get you out of that tree so our secret weapon could make it past the lookout."

The sensor on Neo's vest started blinking. She'd been shot, but not by Kendrick. Gabe had gotten her in the back.

Her smile didn't falter as she let herself melt to the ground.

"Dorian, they're sending Ray for the flag." Kendrick had no doubt Ray was their secret weapon. The woman was as stealthy as her codename, Wraith. And quick as hell too.

He felt his vest buzz. "Ah fuck. I'm down." Lexi sat atop the boulder. Having picked Kendrick off, she was spinning back toward Gabe. They both shot at each other at the same time, aim true. Both were out of the game.

"You two are sneaky," Kendrick muttered. They all had to lie around while the rest of the game played out. No more communication with their teammates.

But talk amongst the dead was okay.

"You two and Wavy sacrificed yourselves," Gabe said. "Drawing us out."

Lexi grinned. "We knew you'd want to eliminate the threats first. We figured Wavy, Neo, and I fit that bill. Ray would've been too obvious."

Neo was still smiling at him from where she leaned up against a boulder. "The only thing we had to make sure of was to get you down from that tree. Reverse psychology for the win."

She'd played him perfectly.

He shook his head, unable to stop his own smile. Damn, this woman was brilliant. And it was sexy as hell. "You really think Ray is going to be able to get past Dorian? Those two basically share the same brain."

Neo just shrugged.

A few minutes later, a soft voice came through all their comm units—the frequency only to be used for an emergency.

Or when a flag had been captured.

"Game's over. Girls win."

"Ray got away from Dorian?" Kendrick asked. He still couldn't believe it.

Gabe began to laugh. "Ray was never their secret weapon. Jordan was. Of course she was."

The quiet one. The one who still struggled with self-confidence even though everyone in the town of Oak Creek had long forgiven her for the sins she and her family had committed.

Lexi and Neo were both grinning as they got up off the ground. Gabe was shaking his head.

"I would've thought she'd take the backup role too. Good for her. Good for all of you ladies for recognizing your strengths and our weaknesses." Gabe pressed a button to talk on his comm unit. "I will buy you as many Electric Smurfs as you want, Mrs. Collingwood."

"Hope you're prepared to drink them too, Mr. Collingwood." Jordan's smile could be heard even through Kendrick's earpiece. "And I can't wait to see you dance."

Neo walked over and held a hand out to help Kendrick up. "Don't worry, Blaze, you still get to see me in my dress."

Chapter 2

"Ladies and gentlemen." Lexi, owner of the Eagle's Nest, stood next to the DJ that had been hired for the night. Her grin was huge as she spoke into the microphone.

She had to start over to get everyone quiet. The dance floor had been cleared except for Kendrick and his capture the flag team, who were currently turned away from the crowd.

Lexi held up her hand to try to quiet everyone again. "Please get your cameras ready so this can be uploaded to as many social media channels as humanly possible. Everybody *get up* for the losers of capture the flag, our own personal cowboys, fulfilling their promise and doing 'The Git Up' Cowboy Boogie!"

The twangy music of the silly song started and the guys turned around. Neo expected them to look a little embarrassed, sheepish. To not know exactly what to do with this performance that had been forced on them.

She should've known better. And knew she was in for a treat when Kendrick winked at her. They hadn't had a chance to talk yet, since the guys were starting the evening off with their promised dance.

A beat passed as the singer on the track told the listeners to get comfortable and grab their loved ones.

The guys didn't do that. Instead, they pulled off their shirts and grabbed cowboy hats.

Neo didn't know a bar in Wyoming could be so loud. She would've gotten closer than her spot at the bar, but she would've had to fight her way through the line of all the *other* Linear guys who were front and center so they didn't miss a bit of the spectacle. Not to mention all the women. It felt like *all* of Oak Creek's women. Word had gotten around.

The crowd quieted for a moment when the guys actually began the line dance.

They all knew it perfectly.

Kendrick, obviously the leader, moved with sexy ease, not at all self-conscious. Baby too. Which could probably be expected from the town's two most charming men.

But the fact that Gabe, Dorian, and Gavin—all former military men with some of the deadliest training on the planet—were up there grinning just as big and moving just as smooth was what brought the house down.

The hoots and hollers—and screams from the ladies—reached deafening levels. Neo couldn't hold back her delighted laughter as the guys did the dance that had become famous on YouTube over the past couple of years.

They did it all: the two-step, the slip 'n slide. They took a sip, slid to the left, to the right. And gave everyone a show they were never going to forget.

Kendrick kept his eyes pinned to hers the whole time. And while Neo had never really been into the whole cowboy scene, Kendrick in that hat with a chest and abs she'd been wanting to sink her claws into for a while now . . .

Save a horse, ride a cowboy indeed.

The dance ended, and the DJ played it again for everyone this time. It was still way too crowded for Neo to head out there, so she enjoyed her drink instead, turning back toward the bar. Especially since the tab was already paid for.

She was in her strappy little dress.

She hadn't needed to wear one tonight to celebrate, but she'd done it anyway. It fell somewhere between keeping a promise and flaunting the spoils of victory.

Plus, she really liked how the bronze and turquoise of the flirty material felt against her skin. And, as promised, the narrow straps showed off her shoulders and the flowy cut of the midthigh skirt exposed just enough leg to keep things interesting.

She might tell herself it had nothing to do with wanting to look nice—to look *feminine*—for Kendrick, but she tried never to lie to herself.

She'd lied to so many other people for so much of her life, it would be too easy to lose any sense of truth if she started lying to herself too.

She smoothed the hem of her dress as she sat on the barstool, enjoying the feel of the soft material. Most of the dresses she owned were for costume more than anything else —from a nefarious past she'd left behind in the last year.

She wasn't exactly sure how she'd gone from hacking and selling information on the dark web to playing laser tag and going drinking and dancing with a bunch of people who were basically heroes. All in the middle of Wyoming.

She only knew that she'd found a place for herself here in the past year that she hadn't known she could *want*, much less find.

"You cheated, you know."

The deep, rich voice whispering in her ear matched the luxurious brown eyes she'd find when she turned around.

And those eyes, that voice, were the biggest reasons she was here in Wyoming.

A smile found her lips without her even trying. "It's not my fault I could predict how you would react, cowboy."

She turned on her barstool. Kendrick was directly behind her. The cowboy hat was gone and his shirt covered that sexy torso, a pity on both counts. But those brown eyes were as fathomless and delicious as they were every time she looked in them. Darker than his skin, which was a beautiful mix of his Asian and African heritage.

More and more lately she'd been getting the urge to scratch her nails along his strong jaw, feel the stubble there. Then run them up over his head where his hair was clipped so short he was practically bald.

She didn't necessarily go for the almost-bald look, but on Kendrick it was sexy. Not at all military. Just a natural way to show off his birthright.

She didn't know what it was about Kendrick Foster that kept her so enthralled. He was older than her by a couple years, but he was so damned likable and charming, with a near-constant rascally little smile, she sometimes felt decades his senior.

Their backgrounds couldn't be more different—his Ivy League education and parents who were both respected in their professional fields. He'd gone to Harvard for under-grad, then Yale for grad school, or maybe it was vice versa, following in *both* parents' footsteps.

Whereas she'd never had much of a family at all. She'd bounced around in the foster care system until she finally figured out how to get herself out. College had never been an option, much less an Ivy League school. Not that she'd been interested.

She worked outside the system much better than she'd ever fit within it.

"You look good, Neoma."

Kendrick had a hand braced on the bar on either side of her.

He definitely didn't feel younger than her now.

Being caged in his arms was just another way he'd been turning up the heat lately. Taking this ongoing dance between them and moving it to the next level.

She liked it.

"If anyone else around here starts calling me that, you're in trouble, Foster."

He grinned. That *I'm adorable and I know it* smile she couldn't resist. He looked down at her outfit. "I've been wondering since the moment you almost caused me to plummet to my death if you'd really be wearing a dress tonight."

"I knew you wouldn't fall." She poked him in the chest. "Just like I knew you would know I was up to something with the text. We needed a way to get you down so Jordan could sneak by. Me texting you was always a distraction—just not the one you thought."

"So very clever. Using Jordan as your secret weapon was, too. Especially when you had Ray available."

Jordan wasn't as fit or as fast as the phenom Ray. But that was why it had worked. Neo smiled. "Ray is definitely a weapon, but she's not a secret. Jordan was perfect."

"You played us well." He leaned in slightly. Not enough to invade her space, but like he wanted to make sure he was breathing the air she breathed. "Dance with me."

" 'The Git Up'?"

"No." He rolled his eyes. "Hopefully, my public dancing career is now over."

"You guys looked good."

"Never let it be said we don't take our promises seriously.

I've even had a couple of Electric Smurfs." He mock shuddered. At least she thought it was mock. Maybe not.

"I've had one too."

He shook his head. "Those things have led to some dangerous situations. They got Zac and Anne together, you know. And Violet and Aiden. I think they might have had something to do with Baby and Quinn also. Dangerous stuff."

She smiled. "I would expect nothing less from blue-colored drinks. But I think we can handle our liquor. Lead me onto the dance floor, as long as I don't have to wear a cowboy hat."

She felt the heat of his hand at the small of her back through the material of her dress. The gesture was respectful and protective—a gentleman's touch.

Everything about his touch drew her in. Hell, everything about him in general drew her in.

Kendrick was all the right kinds of right for her. Sexy and confident, but not pushy. Cocky, but always willing to listen and learn. And so goddamned handsome, even though he knew it.

It might be his looks that drew her like a fly to honey, but it was his brain that kept her ensnared. She'd never known anyone who could match her wit for wit, not only in everyday conversation, but also in all things computerized. Kendrick was hands down the most brilliant person she'd ever known with the keyboard.

Except for maybe her. But that was close enough.

The music was slow as they got to the dance floor, and he turned, holding one hand out for her.

He even danced like a gentleman.

"What's that look for?" He cocked his head to the side as he studied her.

She shrugged. "Nothing."

He stepped closer and slipped an arm around her waist. They began to sway to the sultry beat from the speakers.

People were laughing, dancing, talking all over each other, as this group always did. "Everyone is having fun, even though you guys lost." She held up a finger. "And don't say it was because we cheated."

He let out a bark of laughter. "Fine. You used our weaknesses against us."

"That's shrewd, not cheating."

"Fair enough." He tucked her closer, making her even more aware of the differences between their heights, their sizes. The hard muscles of his shoulder rippled under her fingers as he moved them expertly to the music.

"I glad you're here," he whispered in her ear. "Even if you won."

"I'm glad I'm here too. And glad I won."

He shook his head and eased back so they could see each other's eyes. "If I say you should wear a dress more often, will it get me punched in the gut?"

"Maybe not if you agree to take me out somewhere where it's appropriate for me to wear a dress."

He lost his rhythm.

She looked down at his chest and smiled. She loved that the thought of going out with her could cause this strong, smart, charming man to trip up a little.

She didn't suffer from self-esteem issues. She knew she was attractive, knew what guys saw when they looked at her. Five foot four with hazel eyes and a nice rack. She had curves but wasn't overweight. Her wavy hair fell over her shoulders tonight although she usually had it up in a ponytail or messy bun. Currently blond, although she'd been thinking about going back to her natural brunette.

She was pretty, and accepted that as part of herself. But it had been a long time since she'd let any man close enough to truly care about whether they got a little *tripped up* over her.

Especially since she got tripped up over him just as much.

He started them swaying again. "You know, I've been wanting to take you out for nearly a year."

"But you've never actually asked me."

"Because you would've said no. Or maybe yes. Either way, you weren't ready."

Now she lost her rhythm a little. Was that true? Would she have said no if he had asked her out before now? Or yes for the wrong reasons?

She might've said yes to get information about the town, or the people, or him. Or maybe just to spend a hot, meaningless night with an attractive man and walk away the next morning.

But it wouldn't have been because she really wanted to go out with him. With *Kendrick*.

Evidently, he'd known that even when she hadn't.

"It was worth waiting until you were ready," he murmured.

Had anybody in her entire life thought she was worth waiting for?

Granted, she hadn't been one to stick around and find out. Her entire adult life, she'd believed in being the dumper, not the dumpee.

But here she was in Oak Creek, sticking around. And here he was, waiting for her.

"Ask me now. For this weekend. I'm ready." She stared into those brown eyes as they swayed, commotion and laughter surrounding them but not breaking into their bubble.

He smiled. "Okay, but this is bringing up terrifying memories of my prom-posal in high school."

"What?"

"Didn't you have someone make you a sign in high school to ask you to prom? Prom-posal. My mom still has the most embarrassing pictures of that up in our house."

"No, no embarrassing prom pictures for me." No prom at all. Because she'd been—

Oh shit. He couldn't ask her out for this weekend.

"Okay, fine, no posters. Just a question. Will you go to dinner with me this weekend and wear a dress?"

She was such an idiot. She grit her teeth, wanting to kick her own ass. "I can't."

He stopped their dancing again. His eyes narrowed. "You playing some sort of game here, Neo? Because I'm not."

"No, I'm sorry. Talking about prom reminded me that I have something I have to do this weekend, out of town. Any other time I will take you up on your prom-posal, I promise."

"Fine. Next weekend you let me take you somewhere in a dress."

"Deal." She stopped dancing, stepped back, and stuck out her hand to shake.

He took it, but instead of shaking it, he pulled her closer, putting her hand on his chest and placing his over it. His other arm slid around her waist.

He bent his head until his lips met hers, softly, gently. Like he was learning the shape of her. Like they had all the time in the world.

"Deal." The word was a whisper against her lips.

His lips made their way up her jaw until they were dancing cheek to cheek again. He kept her close and only murmured that she was a cheater once.

A new song started with a faster tempo, and he twirled her around. Of course he was just as good with upbeat music as he was with slow . . . and cowboy line dances.

She'd keep him out on the dance floor with her all night

long—this man who was willing to suffer through scary blue drinks and public dances to honor a bet. To admire her in a dress. To take her out on a date, but only when she was ready.

And even more, to actually know when that was.

Because for the first time maybe in her whole life, she *was* ready.

Chapter 3

Ray Lindstrom wasn't known for enjoying busy places, even a bar like the Eagle's Nest, and being surrounded by friends who were laughing and having a good time. Too many potential threats. Not enough exits. No way for Ray to keep enough weapons on her person to combat every possible catastrophe her mind could think up.

Her own self being the biggest potential catastrophe of them all.

But tonight she set all that aside and trusted in the man sitting next to her in the booth—a human barrier between any peril and her, but also between her and the potential danger she could pose to others.

This man who had saved her in every way someone could be saved.

And, sweet Lord, he had taken his shirt off and done some cowboy line dance in public.

Dorian caught her glancing at him and gave her a little half grin. God, he was still taking her breath away even all this time later—a year and a half after their tiny wedding, but a decade after he'd first won her heart.

"Is that look because you're hoping I'll do a personal version of the Cowboy Boogie for you later?" he asked, eyebrows waggling.

She slid a little closer under his arm that was almost always around her, even when they weren't out in public.

It used to be because she'd needed that arm to ground her. To make sure she knew exactly who and where she was. Time, and some of the best electronics that money could buy, had helped her feel much more secure. So now his arm around her was more out of a habit than a necessity.

She would take it. She would take his big arm around her every day for the rest of her life whether she needed it or not.

"I was actually thinking maybe I could talk you into joining me on the dance floor. As my reward for winning since neither of us is drinking."

His eyes widened, but he was already grabbing her hand and sliding out of the booth, his movements quick despite his huge size. "I will take any and every opportunity to hold you in my arms, publicly or privately, so lead the—"

He stopped as both of them felt the buzz on their matching watches. They both glanced down, then back up at each other.

Proximity warning alarm.

Someone was near their cabin, ten miles outside of town. Nobody should be near their house.

"You ready to go?" he asked her.

She nodded, following him as he grabbed both their jackets from the hooks and tossed hers over. "The good thing about nobody expecting us to show up for social events is that nobody asks too many questions when we leave."

He hooked a heavy hand around the back of her neck and pulled her in for a quick kiss. "They're all glad you're here."

She'd never get tired of his kisses, no matter how often he gave her one. "I'm glad I'm here too," she whispered against his mouth. Glad she'd come and played—that she was able to play.

They didn't want to worry their friends, so they stopped briefly on the dance floor to say quick goodbyes. Ray saw the look Zac Mackay gave Dorian—one meaningful glance checking to see if they needed some help. Dorian reassured his friend they were okay just as silently.

A byproduct of spending years together on the same Special Forces team, and even more years in business with one another, was that words weren't necessary a lot of the time.

Dorian drove as Ray reached behind the seat of their truck and opened a hidden custom compartment in the floorboard. She pulled out the weapons located there—a Glock 19 for him and one of her very favorite crossbow pistols—and put them on the seat between them.

They both already had weapons on their person—shoulder holsters and knives in their boots at their ankles. Neither of them ever went out in public without their weapons. Hell, it was only in the past couple of months that Ray had stopped carrying weapons inside their own house.

Neither of them had planned to need weapons tonight. They hadn't needed them the last time the proximity alarm had gone off either.

"Want to do an earplug test?" Dorian glanced at her for a moment.

As always, she had them in. The specialized pieces of technology that fit into both her ear canals were much, much more than merely earplugs. On standby, they let sound through, but with a press of a single button on her or Dorian's watches, or by hitting a certain pitch with her voice in case her hands were tied, the earplugs went into active mode—blocking all sound to her in three-tenths of a second.

There was also an attack mode, which would lock the device into her ear and let out a frequency that would incapacitate her completely, causing her to lose consciousness.

Fortunately, she'd never needed either setting. Honestly, the entire device was overkill, given that the people who'd tried to control her mind were all dead. But having the earplugs allowed her to live and function with the knowledge that she could never again have her free will stripped from her the way it had been by the people of Project Crypt.

She could never again be forced to hurt someone she loved. Especially Dorian.

And the earplugs were much more functional than the bulky noise-canceling headphones she'd worn the first year she'd been married to him.

They both knew the earplugs didn't need to be tested now—Ray always made sure they were functional. Dorian was offering to test them to reassure her. To give her a feeling of control.

"Yeah. Test from your watch."

He hit the button, and a moment later her world fell silent. She could feel the vibration of the moving truck but couldn't hear it. Could see Dorian's lips move but only knew what he was saying by reading them.

"Good." She could hear her own voice but only because her mind automatically filled in the gaps of what her ears weren't providing.

Dorian pressed the button again and sound came back.

She got out a different earpiece from the weapon container and handed it to Dorian. It also contained a microphone and would allow them to communicate while they checked the perimeter breach.

"Do you think the situation has changed?" Dorian asked,

both to test the communication piece, and because it was on their minds.

She nodded in indication she could hear him through her earplugs. "It has to have changed. It can't be like the last time."

"I'm not sure if that's better or worse, honestly."

Neither was Ray. They'd left the situation alone the last time since they obviously hadn't had all the intel.

Neither of them said anything more as they drove the miles out of town and into the Wyoming wilderness. It was only in the past six months that they'd made their home closer to Oak Creek.

Home being a relative term. Their house might look like a normal cabin from the outside—purposely designed to seem old and small, nothing to entice further perusal. But inside, it wasn't much short of a fortress. It was a place they'd had built for themselves to meet their unique needs—ones most of the rest of the world, who slept soundly in their beds at night without any thought to the multiple dangers that surrounded them, never even considered.

They parked far from their cabin and got out silently. Under almost any other circumstance, the proximity alert would've had them rushing toward the alarm, ready to take out the potential threat.

This wasn't any other circumstance.

"I'll come around from the south. I want to check the sensor, make sure it's working correctly. Something at the river could've tripped it." Dorian was looking out through the trees.

She'd be putting on night-vision goggles in a moment, but not Dorian. He'd spent years in these woods, occasionally for weeks at a time when he'd thought Ray was dead and his PTSD had gotten the worst of him. He had a connection to the wilderness that was damned near spooky.

His code name in the military had been Ghost. The way he traveled in the woods—silently, almost invisible—reaffirmed the name. He didn't need night-vision goggles.

"I'll go straight there." She didn't have to explain where. They both knew where this little party was leading.

He pulled her in for a kiss. "I'll be right behind you."

Ray pulled away and took off in the opposite direction as Dorian. She didn't have nearly his senses when it came to the woods, but she knew where she was going. She was running on land they owned.

They owned all the land around their cabin for hundreds of acres, had bought it up before ever building their home here. There were a few hunter survival shacks on their land, which she and Dorian had chosen to leave alone, setting up motion detectors inside to let them know if anyone was there. Someone using one of the huts didn't necessarily mean a nefarious presence—the Wyoming wilderness was vast and the survival cabins could save someone's life if they were caught out in bad weather.

There'd been no indication of any sort of habitation until two weeks ago when the motion detector had gone off in the hut closest to their own. The one she was sprinting toward now.

She and Dorian had observed but hadn't engaged in any way, thinking it was a hiker who'd decided to take a couple of days to rest, since that hut was in decent condition.

It hadn't been a hiker.

And the hut hadn't been vacated in two weeks.

Then, in the past few days, the proximity alarm to Ray and Dorian's own cabin had gone off three times. The alarm by the river.

Neither Ray nor Dorian took presence in their personal space—all two square miles of it—lightly. They'd both gone into warrior mode, prepared for the worst. Prepared to kill.

They'd both been flabbergasted by what they'd found.

The same thing Ray found again now as she stopped in the darkness behind a tree and used the zoom function on her goggles to look in through the window of the cabin.

Two *children*.

"They're still here, D." She spoke low, but the communication unit picked her words up clearly.

"Damn it. Any adults this time?" Dorian was running but wasn't winded.

"No. Still just the kids."

"I think they were down at the river hunting. That's what triggered the proximity alarm. I found one of their box traps."

She and Dorian had placed a sensor at that particular place because it was the narrowest part of the river. The place someone was most likely to try to cross if they were coming to attack Dorian and Ray.

But it was also one of the best places for fishing and small game hunting.

"What the hell are two kids doing alone this far out for two fucking weeks?" She watched them together now inside the cabin. "Hunting by themselves? Cooking? They can't be much more than ten or eleven years old."

The boy was older than the girl, but not by much.

Ray shook her head. "I don't see any signs of any electronics or vehicles. Again."

How had they gotten here? Why weren't they panicked?

"It's time to get closer, D. I want to hear what they're saying."

"I'm almost to you. Wait until I get there."

"Roger." She didn't mind waiting. She was well aware that there was something highly unusual about these kids being out here alone. In her and Dorian's world, *highly unusual* frequently meant *deadly*.

Their enemies using some kids to trick them into doing something stupid wasn't completely out of the question.

"I want to do a full sweep before you approach the cabin," he said.

"Roger. I'll take the north and northeast quadrants. You get the rest."

That left Dorian with a lot more to cover, but they were way past the point in their relationship where they couldn't acknowledge each other's strengths and weaknesses. He'd be able to cover the other quadrants in the same amount of time it would take her to do her small slice.

They maintained radio silence as they checked the perimeter. When they didn't find anything, they met back up. She peeled off her goggles.

"I'm going to keep them in my sights as you approach." He pulled out his firearm and trailed a gentle finger down her cheek. "You need to do the same. I know they're kids, but . . ."

"I won't hesitate to take them out if it's necessary." She could see the demons in Dorian's eyes. Children had been used as pawns—*deadly* pawns—when he'd been stationed in the Middle East. His team had been forced to kill more than one minor in order to save their own lives and the lives of innocent people around them. She and Dorian had tranquilizers in their guns tonight, but they also had backup weapons with real bullets.

It was the only way they knew how to live.

Ray didn't want to hurt any children, and she definitely wasn't going to shoot first and ask questions later. But neither was she going to allow anyone to hurt Dorian, no matter what age they were.

"I want to find out what's going on with them."

He nodded. "Be careful. I've got your back."

She smiled. "Did you ever think you'd be saying that to me when you had me tied up naked, about to torture me?"

He winced. "Are you going to remind me of that during every argument for the rest of our lives?"

"Probably. But how about later you get me naked and tie me up for the fun kind of torture?"

The demons slipped from his eyes. She cupped his cheek. Even when he'd intended on the bad kind of torture, he still hadn't been able to bring himself to hurt her.

She reached up onto her tiptoes and kissed him. "You be careful too."

They separated, and he disappeared into the night.

She approached the window of the cabin cautiously, checking for any signs of explosives or monitoring devices. After doing a slow loop of the whole building, she came back around to the one small window.

"It looks clear. I'm going to approach."

Staying in the shadows, she lifted her head to peek in from the corner. The window had multiple layers of dirt and dust, making visibility limited. Though this cabin was better than most of the survival shacks in the area, it wasn't meant for long-term use.

She could hear the children inside, barely. They weren't speaking English. "I think they're speaking Ukrainian. Mine is rusty at best."

"Do we have any known adversaries in Ukraine?" Dorian asked.

"Not that I'm aware of."

The cabin was lit only by the fire burning in the fireplace. She recognized a spit over the fire—they'd evidently cooked whatever they'd caught in the trap that triggered the proximity alarm.

Now they were huddled together on a small pile of blankets in the corner that made up a bed. It was hard for her to catch much of what they said. They weren't really talking anyway.

"They're reading some sort of children's book in English. A board book, you know? Like kindergartners read. Something about the moon."

"How do they look? Scared? Anxious?"

She watched as the boy nodded at the little girl as she read, and she turned to beam up at him. Then they both laughed. "No. They look . . . happy. Healthy. Both look relatively well-groomed. Almost like this is home."

Which couldn't possibly make any sense.

She watched them another hour and even let Dorian have a turn after he felt sure the area around them was secure.

Finally, they both slipped back into the darkness and away from the cabin. They walked back home together.

"What kind of kids sit happily in a cabin with no adults and no electricity?" she asked.

He shook his head. "And know how to set traps, plus prepare and cook their own small game?"

Neither of them had any idea. But they were going to find out.

Chapter 4

Kendrick's desk was his home. His realm. His domain.

To the casual eye, his entire office probably looked messy and disorganized. But not to him. He thrived in organized chaos, and his office was a reflection of that.

Thanks to a father who was a judge and a mother who was a surgeon, Kendrick's homelife had been organized and scheduled almost to the minute. His parents were the most brilliant, fair, and compassionate people he knew.

But they'd never been able to comprehend their only son's need to keep everything a little off-kilter. Kendrick needed the chaos, the mess, the *noise*—both audible and visual—to function most efficiently.

So the fact that his desk had two different monitors—as well as a third and fourth screen on the wall behind it—two keyboards, and stacks of books and papers surrounding them would seem messy to most people.

But it was *home* for him.

There was very little he couldn't do on his computer. It had been his point of safety his whole life, especially when he was younger and much scrawnier. Then, it had been his place to escape from anyone who'd tried to make him feel insignificant.

His worries about the cool kids were long gone, but most days he still loved to escape into the screens in front of him, into all the information he had at his fingertips.

And today, the information he was gathering was as critical as some of the rescue missions he'd been part of over the past couple years with Linear. Or at least as nerve-racking.

Where should he take Neo on their date next week?

It needed to be in Reddington City, since he was pretty sure that was where she lived. A town the size of Oak Creek wouldn't interest her much. Worked better anyway since the bigger city provided a lot more options. He loved Oak Creek, but the dining choices here were somewhat limited.

He wanted the date with Neo to be perfect. Wanted her to understand that she was someone worth making a perfect date for.

The woman didn't have self-esteem issues—she didn't take shit from anyone. It was one of the things he most admired about her. But when it came to romance, he had a feeling she was more of a newbie.

He grinned. He was going to enjoy the hell out of showing her—

His phone buzzed on his desk and he grabbed it, hoping the text was from Neo. She'd been gone for two days on her mysterious trip and would still be gone two more. He wanted to talk to her even if only for a few seconds over text.

But it was from Baby Bollinger.

Hi Kendrick. Can you come over to the garage to talk about your car troubles?

Kendrick stared at the text, reading it again. It shouldn't be weird because Baby was Oak Creek's best mechanic.

But . . . Kendrick's car wasn't in Baby's shop. Kendrick

hadn't been having any car problems at all. Not to mention the tone of the text was too formal for Baby. Plus, he hadn't called Kendrick *Blaze.*

The Linear guys had given him that nickname last year when he'd joked about not having a code name like the rest of them. Since he was half Black and half Asian, *Blasian*—shortened to *Blaze*—had been chosen for him.

Baby joked with Kendrick about it every chance he got—so something was definitely off with this message.

Kendrick stood up. He had been around Linear Tactical long enough to know when something was up.

I'll be right there.

It didn't take him more than five minutes to drive his completely functioning car to the Oak Creek garage. He parked and stuck his head inside the big bay door. Everything seemed normal. Two mechanics were working under two different cars.

"Hey, Blaze." Baby opened his office door and waved. "Come on in here so we can talk."

Brows furrowed, Kendrick made his way back. When he spotted Zac and Baby's brother Finn, two of the founding members of Linear Tactical in the office waiting for him, he had even more questions.

"Hey, fellas. We having a party I didn't know about?" Then Kendrick noticed the electronic box not much bigger than a walkie-talkie sitting on Baby's desk. A signal blocker. "Seriously, what the hell is going on?"

Baby leaned on his desk. "Sorry for all the cloak–and-dagger stuff. The town has some extra eyes and ears today, and not the good kind. You're almost definitely being monitored."

Zac reached out to shake Kendrick's hand. "Wyatt's in trouble. Someone nearly killed him yesterday. He snuck into town and needs help with a computer drive that's come into his possession."

Wyatt Highfield was another one of LT's big guns. Kendrick didn't know him as well as he did the other guys since Wyatt took a lot more of the international missions and training.

Kendrick nodded. "Yeah, I got a text from him yesterday on a burner phone. I've been waiting to hear more from him." He pulled his phone out to show to the guys.

This is Scout. I have a gift that needs your love ASAP. Coming to you. More details as available.

The guys all looked at each other. "Evidently, this drive is something pretty damned important. Did you notice any tails coming here?" Finn asked.

"No. I kept a normal eye out since Baby's text was hella weird, but I didn't see anyone."

Finn was leaning against the wall, arms crossed over his chest. "Wyatt let us know that the people chasing him are aware of Linear. He's confident they're already here now—monitoring us, waiting for him to make contact. Is your phone secure?"

Kendrick shook his head. "Some basics, but not anything particularly robust."

"That's what we figured," Zac said. "Bad guys probably know you're here. That's why we've got the signal blocker in play."

"Is Wyatt okay?" Kendrick asked.

Zac shrugged. "Someone contacted him a few days ago and gave him the computer drive. Wyatt doesn't know what's on it, only that it's important enough to kill for."

"Damn," Baby muttered.

Kendrick scrubbed a hand down his face. "What info do we have?"

Zac crossed his arms over his chest. "Guy named Lexington, first name unknown, nearly got the drop on Wyatt in Idaho."

"Idaho?"

"Yeah," Zac continued. "Wyatt was given the drive in Salt Lake City, then went on the run. Bad guys kept finding him, and Nadine MacFarlane took him in, so now she's in the middle of this too."

Finn rolled his eyes. "We're all glad to finally see him with the love of his life, although I wish a life or death situation hadn't been needed to bring them together."

Zac nodded. "Wyatt wants to get this drive to you so you can crack it and he can get Nadine out of the thick of things as soon as possible. She's been through enough."

Wyatt had been half in love with Nadine for the past two years. They all knew he'd been waiting to make his move. Waiting for her to heal enough—physically and emotionally—to be ready to face the world again after suffering a devastating attack.

Evidently, someone trying to kill Wyatt had upped his timeline.

"There's too many eyes all around town now for him to get it to you," Zac said. "We're going to meet at Dorian and Ray's place at eight p.m."

Kendrick grimaced. "Damn it. That cabin is impossible to find."

But he understood why they were meeting there. Dorian and Ray had no official connection to Linear Tactical, so no bad guys would be looking for them. They had no official connection to *anyone* since Ray was legally dead.

But their cabin did make for a good place to meet—whoever was chasing Wyatt would never find it. Kendrick had been there twice, and he wasn't sure he could find it.

"All right, I'll be there. Hopefully."

"Sorry we couldn't tell you this over text or phone," Baby

said. "Wyatt feels certain this guy Lexington and his men have eyes and ears on us."

"So what do we do?" Kendrick asked.

Finn shrugged one large shoulder. "We all act normal until tonight. Then do what we always do: see what we're up against and work the problem."

Chapter 5

The first part of working the problem was finding Dorian and Ray's damned house.

The guys had been right; there had been tangos all over Oak Creek all day. Kendrick had to lose a tail *twice* to get to the cabin, but he'd had help from Baby. Kendrick had gone in the front entrance of the Eagle's Nest and straight out the back, where a second car had been parked.

Of course, finding the Lindstroms' cabin itself, even with precise coordinates, was never easy.

"Seriously, Dorian, is it too much to ask for you to get a house where there are street signs?" Kendrick said once he finally found it and hiked the half mile from the closest road. Dorian let him inside to set up his laptop at their kitchen table. Wyatt and Nadine had arrived too.

Dorian grinned, wrapping his arm around Ray. "You're mad because your specialized GPS couldn't find our place. What's the point in being off the grid if you're not *off the grid?*"

Kendrick rolled his eyes, but it was good to see the big man smile like that. Just like it had been good to have him and Ray play capture the flag. Kendrick could remember a year and a half ago when they'd thought they'd lost Ray forever, and he'd doubted he would ever see Dorian smile again.

Plus, it was Dorian and Ray who'd brought Neo into Kendrick's life, so as far as he was concerned, they could live as far off the grid as they wanted to. The cabin blended into the wooded environment so well, it was almost unrecognizable from the outside—especially in the dark. It was also built partially underground, hiding a great deal of its size.

Kendrick clicked away on his laptop for a few seconds and brought up the info he'd been working on this afternoon about the person chasing Wyatt. "Is this the Lexington who's been chasing you? Zac and Finn mentioned him."

"Yep." Wyatt looked, then grimaced and nodded. He was sitting next to Nadine, the woman burrowed into his side, looking a little overwhelmed. Kendrick couldn't blame her. They'd been through a lot over the past twenty-four hours. Her house had been burned to the ground—with them almost trapped inside it—and the two of them had to run for their lives through miles of wilderness.

"Meet George Lexington. I found lots of fun info about him."

"He's the human trafficker?" Nadine asked.

Kendrick shook his head. "Oh hell no. This guy couldn't organize a Girl Scout meeting, much less a human trafficking network. He's a heavy. A thug for hire."

Wyatt nodded. "All right, so he's no Einstein. That's good."

Lexington definitely hadn't been good at covering his electronic tracks. Kendrick had been able to find out everything about him almost down to the color of his underwear within a couple hours of searching.

He'd wished Neo had been around today to help him

work on it. Not that he needed help hacking someone as dense as Lexington, but this was the sort of thing the two of them bonded over.

White-hat hacking. Something new for both of them—especially her. They both liked it.

What he'd found about the man chasing Wyatt hadn't been pretty.

"He's definitely brutal. He's left a blood trail a mile long. Guy is sadistic as fuck. Sorry." Kendrick gave Nadine an apologetic smile when she stiffened and Wyatt glared at him. "What I meant is, Lexington's not someone any of us want to be friends with. He mostly works around Vegas and Reno but evidently felt it was worth his time for an inter-state pursuit. He's been after the drive—and you—because someone offered him an insane amount of money to get it."

"Who?" Nadine asked.

Kendrick winked at her. "Imma find that out for you right now." He held up his hand. "Drive?"

Wyatt handed the small electronic box to him. It had an external power switch. Interesting. He flipped the switch on.

"Okay, let's see what you've got," Kendrick whispered to the drive as he attached it to his computer and began sorting through the firewalls. He didn't want to do anything to trip security measures on the drive.

The others talking around him was a vague hum that didn't draw any of his focus. It only took a few moments to realize accessing the contents of this drive was going to be more complicated than he'd originally figured.

"Shit." Whoever had set up this drive knew what they were doing when it came to cybersecurity. Infosec—information security—at this level wasn't something Kendrick came by often.

Every method he tried to gain root access to the drive

had him alternating between grimacing and laughing. This little beauty didn't want to give up her secrets.

"I know someone just like you," he whispered to the drive with a smile. "But I'm patient, consistent, and charming. No one can resist me for long, even you."

Neo wouldn't be able to either. He was counting on it.

As he dug deeper into the drive, his smile faded. *What the hell?* An embedded signal in the asymmetric cryptography. That was not expected.

Even worse, the signal was *live*.

He became aware of the other people in the room as tensions changed around him. His friends were no longer idly chatting. Dorian had received some sort of alarm.

"Somebody's out there who's not part of our team." Dorian walked over to where a hutch sat against the south wall of the cabin. But when he opened it, there were no dishes. It was a complex security system showing surveillance, heat signatures, and all sorts of trouble.

No one was going to sneak up on Dorian and Ray unawares. Kendrick wasn't surprised to see the system they had in place, although he was impressed as hell.

Dorian pointed at two blinking dots. "That's Zac and Finn. But someone just tripped our outer perimeter." He pointed to the other end of the screen where dots had appeared.

The guys tried to ascertain if Wyatt had been followed, because there were definitely a number of dots heading toward the cabin from a distance.

Kendrick's attention was drawn back to his computer screen, and he swallowed a curse.

The drive let out another electronic ping. Kendrick had thought it was part of the encryption, but it was an amplified side channel opening for whoever knew to look for it. That was how the bad guys had ended up here—they'd been following the *signal*, not Wyatt.

Shit.

"They found us through the drive," Kendrick said.

"What?" Wyatt turned to look at him. "Is that possible?"

He scrubbed a hand over his head. "That's why it has its own power source. When it turns on, it lets out an electronic ping. If someone like our buddy Lexington knows to look for the ping, it's like a homing beacon."

Everyone was talking again about the plan—trying to figure out the best way to keep out the enemies closing in. Ray and Dorian were concerned about some unsubs out in the woods.

Kendrick turned his attention back to the drive. He immediately shut down the electronic ping so it would no longer give away their location. Not that it helped much now, the bad guys were already here. He cursed himself for not checking for that sort of defense mechanism to begin with. He began checking for anything else of the sort he might have missed.

He was so busy looking for potential threats from the drive that he almost missed a piece of code that changed everything.

He stopped. Re-read. Double-checked that the information was what he thought it was.

It was.

Mosaic.

He stared at the screen in front of him. "Shit."

The drive contained info about Mosaic's inner workings.

The little box had just become a near-priceless treasure. If they could access its contents, it could play a major role in stopping a huge criminal organization.

Kendrick did the only thing he could do right now, even though he didn't want to—he shut his computer down. He couldn't take a chance on accidentally tripping any defense mechanisms that might cause the drive to corrupt its own data.

He looked up to find everyone staring at him.

"We've got bigger problems than Lexington or whoever is after you in the woods right now," he said.

"That can't be good," Nadine whispered.

Kendrick scrubbed a hand down his face. "I know who's paying Lexington to get the drive back."

"Who?" Wyatt asked.

"Mosaic."

Everybody cursed. Mosaic was a criminal organization with a long, ugly reach. Linear had had a close, personal experience with them a few months ago with the near-kidnapping of Gavin's fiancée, Lexi.

"This drive is a much bigger deal than you thought," he told Wyatt. "It contains details on the inner workings of Mosaic. Evidently, they've branched out from treason and cyber terror to actual human trafficking."

Dorian stepped forward. "You need to get this info to Ian DeRose. If it's Mosaic, he's going to want to know."

Kendrick nodded. "He'll be my first call. Ian and the Zodiac team are the only ones who'll be equipped to move on the info."

Zodiac Tactical was a world-renowned private security contractor. They were the utmost experts at security work of all types: risk consulting, intelligence gathering, private and corporate guarding, international hostage negotiation and rescue.

If the law couldn't, or *wouldn't*, handle it, Ian DeRose and his team could.

"Kendrick," Ray said, her eyes narrowed, "do we have Mosaic soldiers outside our door right now?"

"How many people did you detect through your

surveillance system?" He began to disconnect the rest of his equipment.

"Half dozen at most," Dorian said.

"Then it's not Mosaic. If it were Mosaic, there would be a hell of a lot more. It's probably Lexington following the last pings. They don't know what's really on this drive or there would be a lot more."

Dorian nodded.

Kendrick wrapped a cord around his hand. "I hid you as best I could—made it seem like the ping was a malfunction, bouncing all over the place. Once you take care of whoever's out there, your house should be secure again, Ghost."

Kendrick looked back and forth between Wyatt and Dorian. "What's on this drive is time sensitive. Once Mosaic knows someone could potentially access their internal info, they'll come at it no-holds-barred. I need to get it out of here and to someone who can help me. This isn't something I can handle on my own."

"You're going to bring Neo in on this?" Dorian asked.

"She's my best option. Maybe my only option." The only one with enough skill to manipulate this drive without losing the data.

"Fine," Dorian said. "I'm calling Zac so he can get you to safety."

The hell with that. "I don't need a babysitter."

Dorian dropped a hand on his shoulder. "I know, Blaze. But that drive is too important—you're too important—to take a chance with. There's been bad guys crawling around Oak Creek all day. We'd send backup no matter who it was."

Kendrick didn't like it, but he nodded. The important thing was getting this drive out of here and somewhere where he could access it.

By the time Zac made it into the house, Kendrick was

ready to go. Dorian and Wyatt were heading out to the woods to meet up with Finn and neutralize the threat.

Zac led Kendrick silently in the opposite direction, deeper into the woods to where he'd hidden a vehicle. Soon, they were on their way.

Kendrick scrubbed a hand over his face as he stared out the window. "I don't like leaving the Linear guys short-handed in a situation like this."

Zac nodded. "I know. But they can handle it. Protecting and accessing what's on that drive are the most important things. We'll take you to a safe house."

He'd rather work from home, but that wasn't an option. It wouldn't take a genius for someone from Mosaic to figure out that if the drive was in Linear's possession, then Kendrick would have it. "I need a few things from my house if you think it'll be safe. Cracking this drive intact is going to be tricky."

Tricky was such an understatement based on what he'd seen tonight.

"Now is probably the best time before they know you're gone."

They parked a few blocks away from his building. Zac pulled a Glock out of his glove compartment and handed it to Kendrick. "If Mosaic knows you can access their secrets, they won't hesitate to kill you. They've already killed to get this drive back."

Kendrick nodded. He knew enough about Mosaic to take the threat seriously.

"Let's get in and out quick. You won't be back here until this is over, so make sure you get everything you need." Zac put a hand on his shoulder. "Ready or not, your life has just totally changed."

Chapter 6

There were six dead men outside his cabin.

Dorian didn't celebrate the fact, but he wasn't necessarily upset by it either. Especially since neither he nor his Linear friends had done the killing, although they could have.

It was the dead men's own leader, George Lexington, who'd killed them not twenty minutes after Zac and Kendrick had left. He'd done it on purpose as a diversion—trying to create confusion for Dorian and the other Linear guys. Lexington had planned to slip inside the cabin and retrieve the drive, undoubtedly killing anyone there in the process.

He hadn't been counting on Ray in the cabin, nor that she would eliminate him without a single qualm.

Dorian kept one eye on his wife as he talked to Gavin and Zac, finalizing plans for the bodies. It was nearly dawn. Zac had returned after making sure Kendrick was safe and had brought Gavin because of his ties to law enforcement.

Wyatt had left to take Nadine to the hospital to reset her wrist, which had been dislocated during the skirmish with Lexington, but was back now too. The fact that Nadine had dropped unconscious in the middle of Wyatt declaring his love for her had been pretty damned hilarious.

But the fact that Ray had needed to kill a man—even the righteous kill of a bastard like Lexington—was not funny to Dorian in the least.

Not a single person in the room, except for probably Lexington before he'd died, was surprised that Ray had been able to take him so easily. But Dorian was afraid Ray might pay too high of a price for doing what had needed to be done.

He and Ray had clawed their way back to the surface inch by agonizing inch over the past eighteen months since they'd found each other again.

There'd been a time right after she'd discovered what Project Crypt had done to her when he'd thought she was broken for good. She'd spent endless hours staring out the window, giant headphones over her ears, shutting everything out.

He'd wondered if they would ever have any sort of real relationship again. He'd had to accept that Ray as he'd known her might be gone forever. He'd looked into those blue eyes and for so many days there had been nothing but nightmares and hell.

And if it had meant caring for her in some sort of catatonic state for the rest of her life, he'd been prepared to do it. For his Sunray, he would do anything.

But slowly, *so damned slowly*, she'd found her way back to him. He didn't know if he could survive losing her in that way again.

And right now, she was acting odd.

She'd just killed a man with a bowie knife, so *odd* was allowed, but this was different.

She was talking to Finn, wanting to know where the bodies of Lexington's men were.

Dorian slipped up behind her so he could whisper in her ear. "Are you afraid we missed some? That some are still out there?"

She shook her head. "I'm worried about which direction they came from. That maybe they came from . . . by the river."

He knew immediately what she meant. She was worried about the kids. The weight in his chest eased. She wasn't reverting back to a dark place. She was worried that those assholes might have hurt the kids.

Dorian definitely didn't want anybody hurting those children. But honestly, their safety took a back seat to making sure Ray was emotionally intact.

He put both hands on her shoulders and felt her ease back against him. "There's no reason Lexington's men would have come that way. All the main roads come from the south or east. Coming from that direction doesn't make sense."

Finn looked over at them, obviously curious, but didn't press for information.

Dorian would like to check on the kids also. He and Ray had spent time surveilling them over the past couple of days, waiting for adults to show up or looking for any snippet of information on why they were alone in the wilderness of Wyoming.

The kids spoke to each other in both Ukrainian and Russian. Ukrainian was obviously their native tongue, but both were doing their best to speak English. The boy called himself Theo and the girl's English name was Savannah.

When he and Ray had gotten close enough to hear them, they'd discovered nothing helpful. It had all been . . . silly stuff. Jokes and teasing. Singing in both Ukrainian and English. The mention of a grandfather, but no names.

And evidently the book Ray had seen them holding was

their attempt to teach themselves to read in English—something Grandfather had started with them.

But where the hell was Grandfather? Their parents? They'd been alone more than two weeks now.

Ray spun around so she was facing him, putting her back to Finn. "I need to go check on them." Her voice was so low no one else could hear.

Dorian nodded. The sun would be coming up soon. They could make sure the kids were all right.

"I'm going to go see what the plan is for . . . waste removal," Finn said.

Dorian met his friend's eyes over Ray's head and gave him a nod. Finn knew having all these people in the house was hard enough for Ray. He wasn't going to make it any harder by pressing for details on something she obviously didn't want to talk about.

It was part of family's way of looking out for each other . . . knowing when to press and knowing when to ease back.

"I want to make sure they're okay," Ray whispered. "But I also want to talk to them. We need to know what's happening."

"Are you sure us going in personally is a good idea? They'll be able to identify us. We could have Gavin send Sheriff Nelson out to the hut. Say it was an anonymous tip by a hunter or something."

She leaned her forehead against his chest. "Let's check on them ourselves first. Just see. I'm willing to risk it."

He kissed the top of her head. "Okay. Let me help wrap everything up here and we'll go."

She nodded. "I'm going to shower. I . . . need a little time."

He tilted her chin up with a finger. "I won't join you so as not to scandalize my brothers-in-arms, but know I wish I could."

She smiled and took off toward the bedroom. Their dog, Storm, would be back there and would help comfort her. The German shepherd could always tell when Ray needed emotional support.

She didn't say goodbye to anyone else, but the guys didn't expect her to. Dorian walked back over to where they were chatting.

"Ray okay?" Zac asked. "Taking out Lexington the way she did might weigh on anyone."

"She didn't seem to have any problems with that." Dorian shrugged. "There are . . . other factors she's concerned about."

Gavin raised an eyebrow. "Anything we need to know about? Can help with?"

Dorian scratched his fingers along his close-cropped hair. It had been a long night. "No. Not right now. Something we want to look into ourselves. I'll let you know if the situation changes. How's it going here?"

They filled him in. The bodies couldn't be reported here —since Dorian and Ray didn't officially exist according to the government. Gavin was calling law enforcement contacts from Nevada since that was where Lexington had the most enemies. He and Finn were going to drive the bodies to the Utah boarder and stage a scene. Evidently, Lexington had enough enemies that suggesting one of them had killed him and his men wouldn't be far-fetched.

The guys stayed and made sure the kitchen was spotless. Twelve hours after Lexington and his men had appeared on their radar, there was no sign they'd ever been anywhere on or near the property. Dorian and Ray's home was back to what it had been.

It wouldn't erase everything in Ray's mind, but there would be no constant reminders either.

"Thanks, you guys."

Finn grinned. "Hey, family are the ones who help you clean up the bodies."

Dorian shook his head. "I wonder if I can get that embroidered on a pillow."

Wyatt reached out and clapped him on the shoulder. "Sorry we brought the fight to your house, Ghost. That was never my intention."

"If that drive can put an end to Mosaic, it's worth having the fight brought here."

"I'll personally make sure those bodies don't lead here," Gavin said. "I'm going to be doing whatever I can to help Ian take Mosaic down."

Seeing as the woman Gavin loved had nearly been sold to members of the organization earlier this year, Dorian wasn't surprised to hear his commitment to stopping them.

He walked the guys out and said goodbye. When he came back, he found Ray in their small kitchen—but not studying where she'd killed Lexington or even making sure the place was thoroughly cleaned. She was rooting through the cabinets that they used as their pantry.

"Did you change your mind about wanting to go check on the kids?"

"I'm looking for our chocolate bars. I want to take a couple for them. We haven't seen a huge stash of food. I thought they might be excited to have a little treat."

"Yeah. That's smart. Should we take Storm?"

She studied the dog sitting so obediently. He was good with kids—Ethan and Jess loved him to distraction. "Maybe next time?"

"That's probably better. Baby steps." Who knew—the kids might be terrified of dogs.

Dorian took a quick shower and within a few minutes they were out the door, walking toward the cabin. Both of them, as always, kept a careful eye out for anything or anyone out of place. Dorian had his rifle. Ray had multiple smaller weapons.

They did a full sweep of the perimeter of the hut before approaching. Like it had been every time, there was no sign of anyone but children. No adult footprints.

"Are you ready?" she asked after they studied the hut long enough for both of them to realize they were stalling.

"Are you sure making contact is the best thing?"

"We need to find out what's going on. It's September. They can't stay here for the winter. That cabin's not built for it. If they need help, then we have to find a way to get it to them."

"Okay." He squeezed her shoulder. "You go in. I'll cover you from out here." He didn't like sending her in by herself, even though she didn't think there was any danger.

"You're not going to come with me?"

"No. I want to make sure the outside stays secure, but mostly because somebody my size might scare those kids."

Her brows furrowed. "I'm not exactly a child type of person."

He tucked a strand of her blond hair behind her ear. "You care about what happens to them. That's all that matters."

She shrugged. "And I do have chocolate."

"And you have chocolate." He kissed her forehead and slipped his communication device into his ear. "Emergency word?"

She grinned. "Watermelon."

"Nothing like making it more difficult for yourself." They always had an emergency word in a situation where they were separated, a way to let each other know they needed help without giving away that fact to the people around them. Watermelon wouldn't be the easiest of words to work into a conversation, but he had no doubt Ray could do it if she needed to. "I'll have you in my sights the whole time."

She kissed him, then turned toward the hut.

He found a secure spot and watched through his rifle scope as she approached the cabin, knocked on the door, and stepped back. A moment later the door opened a crack.

"Hello," Ray said, her voice clear through the communication device in his ear. "My name is Ray. My husband and I live in a cabin not too far from here. We saw the smoke from your chimney and wanted to come and say hello."

Ray was petite, barely over five foot. With her blond hair and blue eyes, she looked friendly and vulnerable. Many an enemy had underestimated her over the years, assuming she'd be an easy mark.

Not many had lived to tell about their mistake.

But Dorian knew she wouldn't do anything to harm these kids. The fact that she couldn't have children herself, one of the horrors of her past, didn't mean she lacked mothering instincts. She just thought she did.

"If you don't want me to come in, that's fine," Ray was saying. "I understand not wanting to invite in a stranger."

Dorian shifted his sights over to the kids through the crack in the door. The boy was keeping himself between Ray and the little girl. Dorian had nothing but respect for a boy who would put himself between his sister and potential danger.

"I brought you some chocolate." She held out the candy bars. "I know sweet food is the first thing to get eaten up in a long stay. Whenever we see anyone in one of the cabins, we like to bring them sweets."

Smart. Establishing her presence as normal.

Little Savannah pushed at her brother. "Candy," she said softly.

Theo opened the door wider. An invitation for Ray to enter. "Thank you for the candy."

Ray walked inside. "You're very welcome. My name is Ray. What are your names?"

"I am Theo," the boy responded formally.

"I'm Savannah." The little girl stepped out from around her brother.

Ray kept the door open as she moved a little farther into the hut. Dorian knew that was to keep his line of sight open.

"It's nice to meet you, Theo and Savannah. My husband's name is Dorian. He'll be here soon. I'll be glad for you to meet him."

What? Damn it, what was she doing?

He didn't know what her plan was, but that sentence had definitely been an instruction for him to show up.

"Where are your mom and dad? Are they around?"

"No." Theo shook his head. He didn't elaborate.

"Okay. Who is staying with you here?"

The kids looked back and forth between each other. Dorian trained his sights on the little girl. She looked like she was about to cry.

"We live with Grandfather," Theo said. "He will . . . be home soon."

That was obviously a lie, given how Savannah's face crumpled at Grandfather's name.

Ray noticed it too. She crouched down so she was eye to eye with Savannah. "It sounds like you miss your grandfather. It's okay to miss people we love."

Savannah nodded and took Theo's hand. "Grandfather will be home soon." She said it so softly Dorian could barely hear it through his communication device.

Ray stood back up. She didn't press further. "I'm glad.

Want to open your chocolate bars? Dorian will also be here soon."

More instructions. Damn it, he hadn't wanted to interact with the kids at all. Didn't want to scare them. But now he would have to.

He walked toward the cabin as Ray continued to talk with the kids. They weren't forthcoming with a lot of information, so she kept topics light. She found out their ages—eleven and nine.

And she'd been right on track about the chocolate. Both kids had lips smeared with the brown goodness when Dorian cleared his throat from the doorway. The chatter stopped and the kids stared at him.

Ray walked over and put her arm around him. "Dorian, these are my new friends Theo and Savannah. They're staying here in the cabin until their grandfather gets back. Guys, this is my husband, Dorian."

When they didn't say anything, she tackled the elephant in the room head-on. "He's big, isn't he?"

Both kids nodded, eyes wide.

Dorian had no idea what to say. The kids didn't seem to either.

Finally, he went with the first thing that came to him. "I have a dog."

"What kind?" Savannah asked after an amazingly short beat.

He could do her one better. He got out a picture of the German shepherd on his phone and handed it to Savannah.

"Pretty." The little girl touched the screen. "What's her name?"

"It's a he. Storm. He's very friendly. Maybe you can meet him sometime."

Both kids nodded enthusiastically. Guess that answered the question about whether they were afraid of dogs.

And evidently, that was all it took for the kids to decide Dorian was okay. They went back to chatting with Ray. But every time she tried to bring up adult supervision, the kids clammed up. After a couple of times, she stopped pushing.

It wasn't long before he and Ray left, happy to have met the kids, happy to have talked to them.

But with just as many questions as when they'd arrived.

Chapter 7

Neo paid for her coffee at the gas station on the outskirts of Oak Creek and got back in her car. She'd almost gone straight home without stopping for gas, but tomorrow's Neo would want to kick today's Neo's ass when her car was running on fumes in the morning.

And grabbing coffee while there was a no-brainer. It was always time for coffee.

The drive from Oak Creek to Denver was more than eight hours each way, but no matter where she was in the world, she always made the trip to Denver on this particular weekend, or as close to it as possible.

She'd done it for ten years and would probably continue doing it many more, although the address might change. But she would still go. This annual pilgrimage was the only tie back to her childhood—a part of herself she could barely recognize anymore.

She didn't have to physically show up in Denver each year. There were other ways she could gather the information she desired—easier and quicker ways. Most of the time, she used those ways. But once a year she made sure she took in the situation with her own eyes. Even despite the emotional toll.

She put her coffee in the cupholder and glanced in the rearview mirror, caught off guard for just a second by her appearance. Her hair was brown now, closer to her natural color, rather than the blond it had been the past couple of years.

She'd colored it on a whim in the hotel room this weekend since there hadn't been much else to do at night. Keeping her hands and mind busy was important. At one time, she would've gone out and hit a few bars, maybe gone home with a guy, but she didn't have the desire to do that anymore. Didn't have the need to drink herself into oblivion over a past she couldn't change.

But damned if now she didn't look like that not quite seventeen-year-old girl who'd called Denver home for way too long. It was like coming full circle.

And . . . it felt good. *She* felt good.

She sang along with the radio as she drove the last couple of miles to the small house she'd bought in Oak Creek earlier this year. Knowing that Kendrick and their upcoming date was waiting for her had made a stressful weekend much more bearable.

She wasn't ready to tell him where she'd been or why she'd gone there—she wasn't sure she'd ever be ready to talk about it—but knowing Kendrick would be willing to listen made a difference. It had helped her to keep her sights focused forward, rather than drowning in the mistakes of her past.

Kendrick had been helping her set her sights forward since she'd met him.

She grinned. It was time to tell him where she actually lived. She'd made him promise not to attempt to find out on his own, which had been a test on multiple levels. For someone like Kendrick, being told *not* to do something was like catnip—a challenge she was sure he'd agonized over whether to pursue.

He could find her if he tried. There were various ways he could track down where she lived, from physically following her to putting some sort of tracker on her vehicle, or any number of electronic methods he could use to get through the firewalls and VPNs she'd built to protect her home system and hide her IP address.

But he hadn't.

Maybe because he knew she had countermeasures in place that would notify her if he was tracking her. Or maybe —*hopefully*—he meant it as a sign of respect. That he would follow her wishes even though he could *win* this little competition if he chose.

She wasn't surprised to find he'd known he'd be winning a much bigger war by losing this one battle. If he hadn't been smart enough to figure that out, he wouldn't be who she thought he was anyway.

She couldn't wait to see his face when he found out she was only living a few miles north of Oak Creek, not even ten minutes from his place. He probably thought she lived in Reddington City. She'd considered it, but the more time she spent in Oak Creek—the more girls' nights out and get-togethers she was invited to—the closer she'd wanted to be to the tiny town.

This house had been the perfect solution. Close to the action, but no neighbors she had to worry about. Privacy and convenience.

It was home, a word she didn't take lightly. She'd had plenty of places she'd lived, but none she'd actually called *home*. And the feeling had little to do with the house she'd bought and more to do with opening herself up to the people here.

She pulled up in front of her little house, sipping the last of her coffee with a smile. She got out, grabbing her small duffel bag from the back seat, and walked toward her front door.

Maybe she'd call Kendrick tonight. He wouldn't care that it was already evening. They texted each other at all hours of the—

A blow to her back slammed her torso into the side of her house.

She stood stunned against the roughness of the brick much longer than she should have. Partially from the pain, but mostly because the blow—the sheer violence behind it— was so unexpected.

At one time, she would've been on the lookout, would never have been taken off guard like this, even in the short distance from her driveway to her front door.

She tried to push back from the wall but a hand shoved her head forward and pinned her there.

Now she regretted her decision to live so far away from anyone else. At first, she'd loved the thought of having space for a garden and not having to wave to any neighbors. Now she wished screaming her head off would actually do some good.

But damn it, she wasn't going to go down easy if some asshole thought he could assault her and she'd just take it.

She rammed her elbow back into the solar plexus behind her, but the grip on her scalp didn't loosen.

"Careful, Hugo, no marks on her face. But you behave, Neo." The voice came from farther back, not from the person holding her. "We've been scouting this hick town for twenty-four hours looking for you. We thought we were going to have to resort to drastic measures to find out where you lived, but then you showed up at the gas station."

The fact that they weren't here to randomly rob or rape

her was not necessarily good news, not with her past. But it at least meant she was probably safe from serious physical harm.

From the corner of her eye, she could make out the big guy holding her head against the wall, but not the one talking. "What do you want?"

"We need your assistance."

Someone yanked her keys from her hand, not the big guy or the one who'd spoken. So there were three of them.

She heard her front door being opened before the voice spoke again. "Escort Neo inside, Hugo."

Hugo gripped her hair with a rough fist and threw her through the doorway and into her small living room. She spun so she could see everyone, keeping her couch at her back.

"Want me to check the rest of the house to be sure it's secure, Mr. Varela?" asked the second one. The one who'd grabbed her keys.

Varela was the talker and obviously the boss of Hugo and Keys. He closed her front door and nodded. Keys took off toward the kitchen. Hugo remained close to her, ready to grab her if she made a run for it.

Which she definitely would do if given even the slightest opening.

Whatever these guys wanted, she wasn't interested in providing it, no matter what they were paying.

Keys made it back and announced the rest of the house was clear. Neo used the time to study Varela and Hugo without making it obvious she was doing so.

She needed to try playing stupid or weak or both. "I have a couple hundred dollars stashed in my bookshelf, but that's all the cash I have. Just take it."

She lowered her eyes and added a tremor to her voice. It wasn't hard.

Varela tsked. "You know that's not why we're here, Neo."

She gave up the pretense and met Varela's eyes. "Whatever you want me to hack, you're going to have to find someone else. I've developed seizures and am out of the business. Sorry."

Varela walked to her front window and inspected the curtains like he was here to buy them. "I hope not, for your sake. There won't be much reason to keep you alive if you're no longer in the business."

Shit.

She decided to continue her bluff. "Why else would I be living in Wyoming?" That line had worked surprisingly well over the past year.

Of course, none of the individuals wanting to hire her skills had assaulted her or broken into her house. They'd contacted her via the dark web like normal people.

Varela looked over from his study of the curtains. "I concur that Wyoming is a unique place for someone like you to settle."

Maybe this was working. "Yeah." She tapped her temple. "Migraines from staring at the screen. It led to seizures so I moved here to . . . become one with nature and stuff."

Varela tilted his head. "As one does in Wyoming."

"Yes. Exactly." Varela's agreement didn't make her anything but more nervous.

"I'm not going to waste either of our time."

"That's a relief. Wasting time is one of my biggest pet peeves." Her eyes cut to the door. Could she make it before big Hugo grabbed her? She'd learned enough from Kendrick and the Linear Tactical guys to be able to hide out in the woods, cover her tracks, if she could just get away.

But before she could even take a step in that direction, Hugo had her by the hair again and dragged her closer to Varela.

Up close the cruelty in the smaller man's dark eyes was evident. He may not be the person who physically inflicted violence, but he definitely enjoyed it. He was the one with the power to make pain stop—or make it worse.

Varela gave her a smile that held no friendliness whatsoever. "Have you ever made a mistake, Neo? A big one?"

She would've looked Varela right in the eyes even if Hugo weren't forcing her to. "How much time do you have?"

He chuckled. "You're smart. I respect that."

She wasn't so smart that she hadn't ended up trapped in her own house by people who'd kill her in half a second. "What do you want, Varela?"

"I made a mistake. A big one. In my line of business, you don't live very long when you do that."

"You might want to start running then, while you can. Head for Tahiti."

He gave her another humorless smile. "I hired the wrong person for a job last week. George Lexington. He was supposed to retrieve a computer drive so I could get it back to the people I work for. He followed the drive here to Wyoming."

"I'm telling you the God's honest truth when I say I have absolutely no idea what you're talking about. And I definitely don't know a George Lexington."

The thought that this could all truly be a mistake gave her a moment's hope. There was a computer drive missing. She was a hacker. They'd understandably assumed she was part of it.

"Lexington's job should've been easy. That's why I hired him and his men rather than taking care of it myself. Retrieve the drive and return it. Now I have multiple dead bodies to worry about, including Lexington's. And still no drive."

"You probably shouldn't have killed him before getting your answers."

Hugo let go of her hair just the slightest bit, and she shifted as far as possible, which still wasn't nearly far enough.

Varela studied his nails for a second. "I would've killed him, believe me, but unfortunately I didn't get that chance. The police report yesterday said Lexington and his men were killed in some sort of turf war in Utah. But I happen to know he was killed somewhere around Oak Creek. I have reason to believe the drive is around here also."

She gave a one-shoulder shrug. "I don't have it. Pinkie promise. I've been out of town for the past few days."

"But you're not the only computer genius in this tiny town, are you?"

Kendrick. Damn it. She shouldn't be surprised. If there were bad guys showing up dead around here, then of course Kendrick and the Linear team were involved.

She wasn't going to throw any of them under the bus. "Look, I'm not sure exactly what you want from me. I don't really know anybody in this town well. I'm just here to get over my seizures—"

Varela held out a hand to stop her. "Let's cut through the lies, shall we?" He snapped a finger at Keys. "Show her."

Keys pulled out a phone and flipped through pictures of her over the past few months. Pictures of her all over town with any number of people associated with Linear Tactical and especially with Kendrick. Chummy pictures.

She shrugged again. "Yeah, it's a small town. I know people a little. Everybody does."

"I think this is more than a little." Varela took the phone and showed her a picture of her and Kendrick dancing four nights ago at the Eagle's Nest. The image was fuzzy—which meant it had been enhanced. She and Kendrick had probably been in the background of someone else's picture.

The image told Neo a lot. Not the part where she and Kendrick were so intimately pressed together, smiling for one another, but the fact that Varela had it at all.

Someone was scraping images for Varela.

She couldn't tell for certain if it was from public photos on social media, but that would make the most sense. Background images from posted photos could be focused and enhanced, giving away information without the poster realizing it. Getting that info didn't even involve hacking skills.

If *private* photos were being scraped, that would require at least some skill at hacking, but honestly, not much. Most people thought their pictures on their phones were safe from strangers.

Wrong. A skilled hacker could access photos in seconds.

Either way, Varela had someone on his payroll who was getting information for him. He obviously already knew she was close with Kendrick and the others in the photos, so she dropped the pretense.

"Okay, I know them. So what?"

"So you're going to help me with my problem."

She rolled her eyes. "Why would I do that? You've got the pictures. These people are my friends. If you think I'm going to do anything to help you hurt them, you're stupid."

The backhand from Hugo caught her unaware, and she stumbled a couple of steps. But it wasn't the first time she'd been hit in the face. She wasn't going to roll over and start sobbing like some fucking damsel.

Instead, she used the momentum to make a break for the door.

Hugo cursed as she bolted away. Her fingers had barely touched the doorknob, and she thought she was going to make it, when Keys slammed into her, knocking her to the ground in a tackle. He wasn't as big as Hugo, but she couldn't get away with his weight on top of her.

Keys finally rolled off her and Hugo yanked her back to her feet, keeping her arms restrained behind her back.

Varela walked over, shaking his head. "We're not going to hurt your friends, and I'm not trying to hurt you, Neo."

She rolled her eyes. "Right. You'll forgive me if it doesn't feel that way to me."

"You're going to help us. Want to know why?"

She longed to wipe the smirk of his smug face. "Because of the charming personality of Hugo and Henchman Two over there?"

"Porter." Varela smiled again. "You're going to help us or we're going to provide the friends you're so protective of proof that you've been spying on them."

Her entire body went cold. "What?"

"You're not the only one with computer skills. My team discovered that you have recordings of all your so-called friends. Surveillance measures planted to use against them."

All the fight drained out of her. She knew exactly what Varela was talking about.

When she'd first started spending time in Oak Creek a year ago, she'd set up bugs—audio and visual surveillance— all over the place. She hadn't known if she could trust any of them. She'd stumbled onto Oak Creek because of an illegal hack she'd done for Dorian and Ray Lindstrom, for God's sake. She hadn't known what to expect.

She'd taken advantage of the fact that the Linear Tactical people had invited her into their homes. She'd figured if they were that gullible, they deserved to have their privacy violated.

But that was before she'd *known* them. Before she'd known how her life would become entwined with theirs. That they would become people she cared about.

"What will your friends think if they find out you've

watched them eating dinner? Listened to private conversations? Salivated while they had sex?"

She hadn't done that. She'd turned off all the surveillance measures months ago. Even before that, she'd never really used them. She'd just wanted them around in case . . .

In case the people in this town had ended up being less than the friendly, compassionate, tight-knit family they'd seemed to be.

They'd never once been anything but.

She hadn't removed the surveillance equipment because it had been riskier to do so than to just leave it where it was and keep it turned off.

But that's not how they would see it if Varela pointed it out to them. It would be irrevocably damning.

"It's not what you think," she whispered.

He shrugged. "It doesn't really matter what I think, does it?"

No, it didn't. All that mattered was what her friends would think when they found out she'd betrayed them in that way—even if she really hadn't.

What *Kendrick* would think.

"What do you want?" she whispered.

"See, I knew you could be reasonable." He signaled to Hugo and he let her go. "Nobody needs to get hurt. We can be out of your life with no one any the wiser about your indiscretions. You don't really have to do much hacking."

"What do you want?" she repeated.

"Mostly, we need information about a Dr. Claude Sevier. He's one of the world's leading neuromorphic engineering experts, and he created the drive. We need to know if the drive provides any information about where he is."

Neuromorphic engineering. She didn't know a lot about it, only that it was computing and machines that emulated the neural structure of the human brain. A lot of next-level artificial intelligence came from that area of expertise. "Fine. I'll find him."

"We also need you to mislead your boyfriend and make sure he doesn't get any information about my employers from the drive. Any data he does find needs to be corrupted. Then once you discover what you can about Dr. Sevier, the drive needs to be destroyed."

Given all the possibilities, corrupting some data and helping Varela find a missing scientist seemed relatively minor. Nobody got hurt. Her friends never found out what a traitorous bitch she was.

"Okay. I'll do it."

What choice did she have?

Chapter 8

Two hours later, Neo was caught between feeling lucky to be alive and sick for what she was about to do. Especially when she saw the messages she'd missed from Kendrick while *chatting* with Varela.

Evidently, Kendrick had a drive he needed help cracking, and she needed to contact him as soon as she was back in town.

Surprise, surprise.

She didn't call him since Varela was probably monitoring her phone. Not that she didn't plan on doing what Varela asked, but she'd be damned if she'd entertain him by lying to her friends while he could listen in.

She'd driven to Kendrick's house prepared to see him all ruffled and sleep-deprived like he got whenever he was busy cracking something difficult. But he hadn't been there.

So she'd been forced to call him—no answer—and go over to the Frontier Diner to wait for him to respond. She didn't want to go back to her house. She wasn't sure she ever wanted to go back to her house again.

But what if Kendrick didn't contact her right away?

What if he'd already cracked the drive on his own and was off saving the world like the good guy he was?

What would Varela do? Kill her? Tell everyone in town what she'd done with the surveillance equipment?

She needed a plan for leaving town. How stupid was she to not already have one in play? Everywhere else she'd lived, she'd had the literal and electronic equivalent of a bug-out bag already filled with necessities for a complete restart at a moment's notice.

But not here in Oak Creek. She'd gotten complacent. Comfortable. That comfort was going to cost her everything —maybe her life.

"You're going to get me fired if you keep growling into your coffee." Wavy Bollinger slid in on the other side of the booth.

Neo shot her a half smile. "As if."

Wavy was a fixture at the diner, had worked there for years. Nobody was going to fire her. She was also one of Neo's favorite people. She'd been the most inclusive of Oak Creek's residents from the beginning.

"You okay?" Wavy asked. "Nice hair, by the way."

"Thanks. But yeah, it's been a rough couple of days." Neo took a sip of the coffee that wasn't the problem at all. She didn't even bother to point out that Wavy had paint in her own hair. Wavy had paint in her hair or somewhere on her body at any given time. The woman loved her art.

"Aw, did you miss Blaze as much as he missed you and it's made you all cranky? That's so sweet."

Neo wished that was all it was. "Have you seen him around? He messaged me for computer help. I went by his house but he wasn't there."

"I haven't seen him for a couple of days. Finn mentioned there was some sort of brouhaha. Bad guys, evil organizations, that sort of thing." She shrugged one shoulder and grinned. "The usual."

"Yeah, I think said brouhaha is what Kendrick needed my help with."

"And he's not at his house chained to his computer?"

Neo took another sip of her coffee. "Hard to believe, but no. I called him. I'm waiting for him to get back to me."

Plus planning her escape in case she had to run for her life. Maybe she should leave right now. Get in her car and never look back.

It wouldn't be the first time she'd reinvented herself from nothing. Varela might think he had her trapped, but he didn't. Even without her bug-out bag, she could disappear in a way that meant no one would ever find her again.

But it meant walking away from Kendrick without another word.

Ever.

She couldn't bring herself to do that unless there were no other possible options.

"How about if I grab you some pie." Wavy grabbed her hand, giving it a gentle squeeze. "Pie makes everything better."

Neo nodded and watched the other young woman slide out of the booth, wishing pie would solve all her problems. Wishing pie would solve *any* of her problems.

The Frontier's pie, as good as it was, didn't make her feel any better. She forced herself to eat it one small bite at a time, every tasteless swallow a reminder that this might be the last time she had the diner's famous dessert if she had to bolt.

By the time she'd finished force-feeding herself the pie, Kendrick still hadn't contacted her. Maybe that was better. Was she strong enough to make the definite cut? Walk away without a word? Maybe this was a sign from the universe to do exactly that.

The universe had never done her many favors anyways.

She pushed her empty pie plate away and got up to pay Wavy. She still wasn't interested in going back to her house, but there wasn't much point in staying here. It had never taken Kendrick this long to get back in touch with her.

It wasn't like she expected him to drop everything to talk to her, but that was sort of how they'd established themselves with each other. One messaged or called and the other was quick to respond.

But not tonight.

"How much do I owe you?" she asked Wavy at the register.

"No charge. But would you mind running these boxes out the back door? Just stack them next to the dumpster, and I'll break them down for recycling later."

Neo would rather have just paid for her food, but she wouldn't say no to Wavy, so she rolled her eyes and grabbed the boxes.

Wavy grinned at her, all light brown hair with auburn highlights and big green eyes dancing with mirth. So charming and fun, just like her brothers. Everybody loved her.

Including Neo. So she stacked the boxes in her arms.

"You can thank me later!" Wavy called out as Neo walked with the boxes stacked high enough that she could barely see.

"Whatever," she called out. "I'm not coming back in here for a second load."

"Oh, I know you're not," Wavy responded, walking across the diner to take an order.

Neo waved at Nolan, the Frontier's cook, as she cut through the back kitchen. He was rocking out to whatever music was playing over his headphones and barely gave her a wave.

The sun was slowly setting over the Tetons that surrounded Oak Creek. Normally, she would've taken a moment to appreciate it. The beauty encompassing the town was something she'd been in awe of from the beginning.

But not today. She'd rather just stare at the cardboard boxes in front of—

"Thank God you're here."

Kendrick. The relief that poured through her at his voice was almost a tangible thing. She'd honestly thought she was going to have to leave without ever seeing him again.

She peeked around the boxes. "You waiting out in the back alley hoping to mug somebody?"

He took the upper stack of boxes and put them next to the dumpster. She loaded the rest.

And immediately found herself yanked into Kendrick's strong arms.

She couldn't help it, she wrapped her arms around his waist and leaned in for the hug.

"You are not going to believe all the shit that went down while you were gone. It seems like every time we're separated, the world moves into crisis mode around us."

She leaned back so she could look up into his brown eyes. "Nobody was kidnapped, were they?"

"Crazier. And even worse, the people I need help with are the same ones that kidnapped Lexi."

Neo ignored the cold knot of dread forming in her gut. No one was going to get hurt, that was what mattered. She needed to focus on that detail, nothing else. "What are you doing out here?"

"I've been working at a safe house. This computer drive . . ." He shook his head. "It's bad news. I need help. Wavy let somebody in LT know you were here. They knew I needed you as soon as you got back in town." He tugged on a strand of her hair. "Nice. Suits you. I love it. Come on, you're going to want to see this drive."

Only Kendrick would light up like a kid at Christmas when he talking about a nearly unhackable drive. He was so enthusiastic about *everything*, always the opposite of her.

She stiffened. Was she really going to do this, deliberately sabotage his attempts to crack this drive?

His arms slid from around her. "Hey. I'm sorry. I didn't even think about the fact that you've just gotten back in town. Do you need some time to decompress or something? I shouldn't assume you can drop everything and come work on this with me."

But that was how they'd always operated. Normally, she would've raced him to the drive. "No, I want to help. Let's get going."

He slid his arm around her as they walked out the back parking lot. They hadn't gotten far before a truck stopped next to them and Kendrick ushered her inside.

Gavin Zimmerman smiled at her from the driver's seat. "Hey, Neo."

She forced herself to smile. "Hi, Redwood." She called him by his Linear Tactical code name in an attempt to keep things as light and normal as possible.

"I'm only your short-distance taxi. Aiden is waiting on the outskirts of town. Then you'll switch again, and Zac will take you the rest of the way."

They were taking this safe house seriously.

"Are Wyatt and Nadine doing all right?" Kendrick asked. "I've been buried under this drive. I know they both were injured."

She didn't know Nadine at all, and Wyatt was the Linear Tactical member she was least familiar with.

Gavin nodded. "Wyatt is laying low so they both can

recover from their injuries. We appreciate you guys working on this thing. There's a lot of dead people surrounding it, so it's got to be pretty damned important."

The cold knot of dread got bigger.

Kendrick grabbed her hand and gave it a squeeze. "I'm not too proud to say this bastard has me stumped. But Neo and I have yet to find anything computer related that we can't crack together."

Gavin nodded. "That's what we're hoping."

She sat between the two men who believed she was here to help and wished she could dissolve into the floorboard.

The journey the rest of the way to the safe house was as cloak and dagger as Gavin had suggested it would be. By the time they'd finished driving in circles and taking sudden turns in three separate vehicles, Neo wasn't sure she knew where they were.

The safe house was a small, unassuming townhouse on the outskirts of Reddington City. Zac had done the last leg of driving and pulled up in front of it.

"You've got supplies, food. It's even got clothes stocked in your size, Neo." Zac shot her a smile and hooked his thumb at Kendrick. "We made sure you'd have what you need, knowing this one couldn't do much without your brilliance."

"Hey." Kendrick sulked with a grin—something only he could pull off. "I resemble that remark."

Zac and Kendrick did a quick run-through of the house to make sure it was secure, that there were no enemies inside.

It never occurred to them to look for the one they'd brought with them. She tried to ignore the ever-growing knot of dread.

They came back out and Zac prepared to leave. "Good luck, you two."

Kendrick winked at her, then turned to smile at Zac as

the other man got back into his car. "With both of us on this, I'll bet it only takes us twelve hours, tops."

THIRTY-SIX HOURS LATER, the knot of dread had tied up her entire person.

She should've never agreed to this. She felt like the biggest jerk on the planet.

Kendrick was pacing back and forth in the small kitchen, teeth grinding, alternately scratching his fingers over his nearly bald head and scrubbing them down his face. He'd been doing it for hours.

He was not a man who was used to this level of failure, or probably *any* level of failure. Especially not at something he was putting all his effort toward.

The fact that she was the one who had reduced this strong, proud man into a pacing, frustrated shell ate at her like acid in her gut.

"I don't get it. Security on this drive is exceptional, but we should've been able to crack it by now. It's like whoever developed it is inside my brain and knows every single thing I'd try."

That was because she'd worked with him long enough to know everything he'd try. And to thwart it.

She was sitting on the couch in the small living room with her laptop on her lap. His was currently resting on the coffee table, next to the drive. "Maybe you should get some sleep. You know how it is. The brain needs a break, then you can come at it fresh."

He rubbed his eyes. "Every second that I can't figure this out, Mosaic is hurting somebody else. Maybe someone's killed. Sold. I don't want to sleep."

Mosaic.

That was the frozen center of the cold knot of dread in her chest. She'd had no idea that was who Varela worked for. She was just beginning to figure out how bad this organization was.

Kendrick began pacing again, and she couldn't stop herself from setting down her laptop and walking over to him. She wrapped an arm around his shoulders. "You're doing everything you can. That's all anyone expects."

"It's not enough." But he wrapped his arms around her waist, yanking her close, and buried his face in the side of her neck.

As if being close to her gave him strength. As if breathing in the scent of her skin would help him focus, help him solve this problem.

Two days ago, she would've agreed. Would've done anything to help him. Hell, without her sabotaging his efforts, he would've been much further in cracking the drive and secure in his status as computer wunderkind.

"It's going to be okay," she whispered. But the pit of her stomach was telling her the opposite.

He held her close for a long minute before finally taking a deep breath.

There was a healthy dose of renewed determination in those brown eyes when they met hers. "Okay, enough pity party. I'm not sure what I'm missing, but I'm going to find it, and we're going to crack this fucking thing."

Nothing kept him down for long. It was one of the things she enjoyed most about him.

He grabbed her by the waist and spun her around, then propelled her back toward their computers. They'd made a nest of sorts for themselves, surrounded by the equipment they needed.

Any other time, this would've been heaven—just Kendrick, computers, and a hefty challenge in front of them.

The fridge and pantry were stocked, no one was bothering them, and there was an industrial-strength cappuccino maker that rivaled any coffee shop.

Literally her dream.

Instead, she'd spent the past day and a half deleting or corrupting info every time he'd gone to the bathroom or to get something to eat. Fooling Kendrick without leaving any traces had required every bit of skill she had.

He nudged her down onto the sofa and plopped down next to her, grabbing his laptop. "Let's go over it again. As far as we can tell, the drive belongs to and was restricted by Dr. Claude Sevier."

With Dr. Sevier, as per Varela's instructions, she'd allowed Kendrick free rein.

"Fifty-seven-year-old neuromorphic engineer who has worked in France for the past thirty-three years, but was born and raised somewhere in Eastern Europe," she continued for him.

Kendrick squinted at his screen like it contained the answers. "No information about his past eighteen months at all. It's like he stopped existing."

"Except we know the data was placed on the drive within the past few weeks, so he definitely still exists." This had been info she'd passed on to Varela.

"So maybe eighteen months ago is when he started working for Mosaic? That's why he dropped off the grid?" Kendrick shook his head. "There's nothing about his early career that looks like it would link him to any sort of criminal organization, particularly not one like Mosaic. He's always been very well respected in his field. The stuff he's doing in AI—the blend of human and computers— is downright impressive."

She shrugged. "If Mosaic is so bad, maybe they're blackmailing him or something. Forcing him to do what they want."

Didn't that sound familiar?

Kendrick grimaced. "Definitely a possibility. But ultimately, that doesn't matter when it comes to the drive. We've got to figure out how to access it. Which we need his DNA to do safely."

They'd discovered the tiny DNA sensor on the drive yesterday. Given Dr. Sevier's expertise in AI, the creative backup security measure wasn't surprising. Most people attempting to hack the drive would've missed it entirely.

"And the fifteen-digit alphanumeric code. Don't forget that," she added.

Kendrick rubbed his eyes. "Regardless of whether Dr. Sevier developed the drive to help Mosaic or to destroy them, we still need the DNA and code if we want to access the drive without taking a chance on it corrupting its own data. We cannot do anything to hurt that information."

"Right." Except for the fact that she needed to destroy it.

"Are you up for running through everything we've tried again to make sure we didn't miss anything?"

"Absolutely." She forced a smile.

"You're the best." He leaned over and kissed her gently, then rubbed his thumb along her bottom lip. "Let's get this thing cracked so we can go on our date."

He let her go and turned back to his keyboard.

All she could do was the same, hating herself more with every passing second.

Chapter 9

Kendrick couldn't figure out what the hell was going on. It was like one step forward and three dozen steps back.

He had attended two separate Ivy League colleges—one for his bachelor's degree and one for his master's—and never had difficulty with a single class. He'd worked on and cracked some of the most highly sophisticated computer systems in the world. Hell, companies worldwide hired him to make their systems more hacker-proof. One of his favorite jobs was to be on a red team—someone paid to attack a system and discover its vulnerabilities.

There should be nothing about this drive that could keep him from making *any* progress on it whatsoever. Especially not with him and Neo working on it together.

But for whatever reason, every single thing he tried was futile.

And if possible, it had gotten worse since Neo had arrived, even though she'd been right next to him, putting her considerable brain power toward the same endeavor. At least she didn't seem as frustrated as him about their lack of progress.

She'd been the one to discover the breakthrough with Hemingway Travel Agency. Granted, that had more to do with Dr. Sevier—damn near every breakthrough they'd had concerned Dr. Sevier—but it was at least something. Both he and Neo had agreed that a tiny boutique travel agency with only two full-time employees should not have the extreme firewalls in place he and Neo had found.

Hemingway Travel Agency was hiding something, or, more likely, was a front for something. It hadn't taken them long to realize they needed to be on-site to ascertain what Hemingway was hiding. An evil maid attack—accessing the system from the inside.

The travel agency wasn't great progress, but at least it was something and opened up new avenues for Kendrick to consider. Hemingway definitely had something to do with Dr. Sevier, so maybe bringing the drive on-site would give them a clue for accessing it without the DNA and code. Or at least give them a hint as to what the code was since there were 1.5 trillion possibilities.

Sitting in the safe house was getting them nowhere, so he and Neo had decided to break into the Hemingway office. It was three a.m., and they were both sick of staring at the screens and getting nowhere.

They didn't know what they would find, so Kendrick had pieced together a hack that would allow them to quickly run configurations based on the known parameters of the drive once they were in the office. It wasn't his prettiest work, but it would suffice.

Besides, he had bigger things to worry about than attractive hacking, since they were about to literally break into a building in downtown Reddington City. Like, real go-directly-to-jail stuff if they were caught.

"Are you sure your Linear buddies aren't going to get pissed about this?" she asked as they made their way from the safe house down the block to the emergency getaway car.

"I don't plan to tell them. If ever there was a case for the ends justifying the means, this is it." He was sure nobody on the Linear team would applaud them breaking into a building in the middle of the night, but the guys would probably be more upset that they hadn't been in on the action than anything else.

But still, if Neo didn't want to take this chance, he definitely wasn't going to force her. He glanced over at her. "Listen, if you're having second thoughts, I totally understand. I'm sure I can do this by myself."

She shot him a smile as he started the car, and they pulled off into the dark street. "Oh, I'm in. No way you're getting all the excitement by yourself. Field trips are the best part, right?"

"Hell yeah, they are."

He was glad to see her a little more relaxed. He couldn't quite put his finger on it, but something about her had seemed out of sync since she'd arrived.

Of course, everything about this damned computer drive was off. But he could swear there was something going on with Neo too.

He only recognized it because they'd done so much work together over the past year. She'd proven herself indispensable over and over. Neo had been integral in Lyn Zimmerman's rescue when she'd been kidnapped last fall, then had helped the team stop a terrorist in Egypt who might've killed them all, followed by single-handedly providing the intel to rescue Lexi when she'd been taken a few months ago.

Neo didn't crack under pressure. She worked with a quick and calm focus that was admirable.

But for the past couple of days she'd been . . . off.

Maybe it was personal. Was it because the two of them

were going on their date soon—and that was damn well going to happen once this was over—and she knew that was a step in a definite direction. She might be nervous.

Or it could be that last week's mystery travel plans had her distracted. It had taken damn near every ounce of his self-restraint not to dig deeper into where she was going and what was she was doing.

Whatever it was that had her off her game, he wasn't going to push it. She was here solely as a volunteer. And now he was about to ask her to do something that could lead to real-life jail.

And hell, Neo at fifty percent mental capacity was better than most people at one hundred percent, so he'd take it.

"You okay?" she asked as she drove. Her voice was carefully neutral, which wasn't unusual. She was as guarded as he was outgoing.

"Just trying to wrap my head around how to crack this damn thing." Which was the truth, even if she would think *damn thing* meant the drive, not her.

She shrugged one small shoulder. "Some things can't be hacked. Even by the best. We both know that."

That was what he was afraid of—with her, not necessarily with the drive. "I'm not going to accept that. Not yet. I think it'll just take coming at it the right way with the right skill set and the right amount of determination."

She didn't respond.

Hearing her say the drive was unhackable seemed unnatural to him. She was the most talented hacker he'd ever known, had a natural ability he'd never have.

Their styles, the ways they approached problems, were opposite. He absorbed information, then his brain allowed him to take the knowledge and extrapolate from it—growing his own abilities. He'd learned how to work computer systems by studying them and expanding his knowledge.

But her ability was innate, a natural part of how she thought. He wasn't sure if his Ivy League computer science classes would've improved her abilities or merely driven her crazy. Regardless, she didn't need them. When it came to computers, she was one of the most gifted people in the world.

Some things can't be hacked.

Hadn't they both laughed at advertisements where cybersecurity companies claimed to make their clients' information unhackable? Hadn't they taken perverse delight in hacking into those very same cybersecurity companies, showing them how vulnerable they were?

"Everything is hackable," he murmured.

Yet she'd just said otherwise.

He refused to think they'd met their match in this drive. Whatever was going on with it, between the two of them, they were damn well going to crack it.

They parked a couple blocks from the building that housed the travel agency and pulled out their laptops.

"Hemingway Travel Agency," she said. "First floor. Southeast corner."

The building had three floors. The second and third floors contained a lawyer's office, two accounting firms, and a credit union. The other two offices on the first floor were for a modeling agency and a realtor.

"Modeling agency," he said, shooting her a grin. "Maybe we should break in there instead."

She rolled her eyes. "Let's check out what security we're dealing with to get inside."

"I'll check if there's any CCTV feeds we need to worry about."

"Electronic keypad at the building door and the travel agency door. Shouldn't be a problem circumventing those."

He nodded. "Looks like we've got some video feeds, but

they don't seem to be broadcasting anywhere, so no one is watching it live. I'm going to run interference with those so they don't have any record of us being inside."

"Smart."

He was about to cut the closed-circuit feed entirely, knowing it would probably take whoever monitored it at least a few hours to realize there was an issue, when something on the feed caught his eye. "Holy shit."

"What?"

He spun his laptop so she could see the image on his screen, where two guards were walking.

"Are those automatic weapons on their backs?" she whispered.

"Somehow I don't think that's for the modeling agency." There was no reason there should be shoot-first-ask-questions-via-seance security personnel for any of the businesses in the building.

Someone was hiding something big somewhere in that building. And Kendrick was convinced it had to do with the Hemingway Travel Agency.

"Are we sure we want to do this?" She looked over at him. "Those guns aren't pretend. We're talking about more than spending the night in jail now."

Fuck. She was right. He scrubbed a hand down his face. "If we wait, get the team, we're going to lose at least twenty-four hours. Mosaic already knows we have the drive. It'll give them extra time to fortify."

She nodded. "I agree. This is our best shot if we want more info about Dr. Sevier."

"And cracking the drive."

She nodded. "Right. Of course. The drive."

"Then let's do it."

She picked up her computer and began typing. "I'll get

the door codes and rewrite the security program to make sure our entrance won't trigger anything."

He grabbed his laptop. "I'll reroute the CCTV images to my phone so we know where the guards are."

Now it felt like they were moving in sync again. They both worked silently. He finished before her. She was still clicking away.

"Want me to rewrite some of it for you?" How many times had they passed each other their computers, both of them able to take over for one another without any break at all.

But she jerked back from him. "I've got it."

Okay, maybe not in sync.

It didn't take her long to finish, and she shot him an apologetic smile as they got out of the car. He smiled back. He should cut her some slack, considering they were not only about to commit a felony, but they were also going to be hiding from armed guards with psycho guns as they did it.

He kept Neo between him and the wall as they approached the building, not that his body was going to offer much protection from a bullet. Here's hoping he didn't get them both killed. That would not make for a good first date.

He kept an eye on the guards through the security feed on his phone and signaled to her when the guards were the farthest away. They both held their breath as she hacked the rest of the way into the electronic lock, hoping the patch she'd rewritten in the car would hold.

It did, and they were rushing down the hall a few seconds later, not an alarm to signal their arrival anywhere.

They wasted no time getting to the Hemingway Travel Agency door. Once again, Neo's computer voodoo worked perfectly, allowing them to slip inside with no issues.

He squeezed her shoulder as he came in behind her and closed the door. He should've never doubted her.

The inside of the travel agency was nothing like what he'd expected. It was . . . *normal.* A couple of desks with standard computers on them and a filing cabinet next to a couch in the main room. The second office in the back revealed the same, plus a small bathroom.

He wasn't sure what he'd been expecting—wall panels full of bomb countdowns or secret surveillance—but this definitely wasn't it.

Neo looked as disgusted as he felt. "Talk about anti-climactic."

"Let's hope we can find something in their system."

He hooked up his computer to the one on the desk. His laptop would serve as a bypass between that unit and the drive. He traced his finger down the black box.

This time, he wasn't going to be stopped.

Chapter 10

Kendrick grinned down at his computer. Everything was going the way he wanted it to, and he was making progress. *Finally*.

The travel agency's firewall was as serious as the weapons the guards carried. But here on-site, Kendrick knew he'd be able to crack it and had been working steadily toward it since sitting down.

The first couple layers of security could've been hacked by a determined toddler. He was through those in under thirty seconds. He glanced at his phone. No sign of the guards.

The next two layers he peeled through easily too. They were good, about what he would've expected from a company that did a majority of their business online and needed to keep information safe. Enough to keep out most script kiddies—the would-be hackers who had enough computer savvy to be pains in the ass, but not enough to do true infosec harm.

But it definitely wasn't enough to keep Kendrick out. "That's right, come to daddy."

Neo looked up from her computer. "Success?"

He winked at her. "No one can resist my charms for long. Give me five more minutes, and I'll be under her skirt."

He expected Neo to laugh—they used inappropriate dirty talk all the time when it came to hacking. But she just went back to what she was doing.

Because she's focusing on the problem, asshole, not on being cute. Do the same.

The final two layers of security proved beyond a shadow of a doubt that something was going on in this system that went way beyond a travel agency, not that he needed further proof. These layers took a lot more focus. He muttered under his breath at the screen as he worked faster than the system to successfully get around the firewalls.

This was it. They were finally going to get some fucking answers. Once he was through this security, he'd be able to use the system to access the drive.

But a few seconds later, he was stopped dead in his tracks.

"What the actual fuck?" He blinked at the screen as a new line of protection seemed to pop up out of nowhere.

"What?" Neo stopped typing. "Are you in?"

"No. Bastards just hit me with a Trojan horse on their own system. I'm blocked out." He hadn't been expecting that.

"Did their IDS catch you?"

"No, I bypassed it." He'd known to look for an intrusion detection system. It had been part of the "normal" level of security he'd been expecting.

But this Trojan horse? There was no way he'd be able to get around this in time. It would take hours.

He rubbed the back of his neck, jaw clenched. It didn't make any sense for them to use that method of security, and for it to pop up at the last second.

"Why did you do that?" he whispered to the screen.

Why use a nontraditional method of security when there were a dozen more logical and, in the long run, more secure ways to protect the info on their system? The Trojan horse would keep him out now from the particular direction he'd been coming at the info, but it didn't help security overall.

He began chipping away at the outer shell of the Trojan horse, careful not to leave any digital fingerprints that would give him away. The more he saw, the more impressed he became. He whistled through his teeth. Whoever had set this up was fucking smart. This was more than standard security.

"We may have a new player," he said as he typed.

"Why?" Neo's fingers didn't stop either.

"How would anyone besides you and me even think to use a Trojan horse to secure the system from an evil maid attack? In almost one hundred percent of cases, it's not worth the effort, and even the best infosec experts wouldn't find it worth their while to utilize. Too many chances of it backfiring."

Now she stopped typing and looked over at him. "What are you trying to say?"

"I was coming at the info from a direction very few people would've thought of, much less have the expertise to pull off. The Trojan horse is one of the few things that could've stopped me. So I'm wondering if there is some new, high-level player we don't know about. One working for Mosaic that thinks like us."

The elite hacking world was small. Insular. There were only maybe a dozen people in the world at his and Neo's level. They all knew each other virtually, or at least knew of each other's signatures and preferred methods.

It wasn't a club, exactly. More like a masquerade ball where everyone was identifiable by their masks and costumes and dance style, but the person beneath was unknown.

"New player. Right." She nodded. "What are you going to do?"

"I'm not sure."

He turned back to his screen. First thing he wanted to do was figure out what he could about who he was up against.

Want to play, new Mosaic guy? Tell me a little about yourself, you smart bastard.

Instead of trying to get around the Trojan horse, he gathered information about it. He had the data he wanted a few seconds later.

He stared at it. That wasn't possible. "Oh shit."

"What?"

"The Trojan horse was added to the system in the past twenty minutes. Why the hell would they do that if they didn't know we were coming? And if they knew we were coming, why are we not facing down the machine gun guards right now?"

"Shit. I don't know. Do you think—" Something beeped on her computer. "Wait, I've just gotten something on Dr. Sevier."

Kendrick nodded, letting her work, still trying to wrap his head around the timing of the Trojan horse insertion. At least she was making some progress.

"Sevier was booked on a flight from Belarus to Salt Lake City three weeks ago. From there he was supposed to transfer to Los Angeles, but he never made it onto that flight."

"Any intel on where he is?"

She shook her head. "No, but I have an updated photo of him. That provides options for searching."

"Anything that would help with the alphanumeric code?"

"I'll keep looking," she said. "We still okay with the guards?"

He glanced at his phone. "No sign of anything out of the ordinary."

"You should focus on Sevier too. If there's a Trojan horse, you won't get around it in time to access the drive. Let's worry about Sevier first, then figure out all the other crazy later."

"Yeah."

But now that he knew he was dealing with someone who thought like him, it changed how he would come at the drive. That may have been his problem all along—overthinking it. Attempting to access the drive in a way no one else would anticipate.

He'd been coming at it sideways, the way he came at most infosec projects—a mix of traditional hacking and his own special blend. That evidently wasn't smart enough, so he needed to think in a different way.

Or . . . maybe he merely needed to knock on the front door, so to speak. Strong-arm hacking wasn't his style, it lacked any finesse, but it was worth a try.

He quickly coded a program that would brute-force random codes at the drive, borrowing from a denial-of-service attack in which hackers tried to crash a website by overloading it with info.

If the drive wasn't connected to its home root system here in the office, a DoS remote electronic beating like this would cause it to shut down to protect itself and corrupt the data. But because Kendrick was already inside the root system, the drive read his pings as more information being downloaded.

No one was more surprised than him when it actually began to work. He laughed out loud.

"What?"

"You're not going to believe what's working. A brute force hack." It was Hacker 101. "The drive is reading my pings as information to be downloaded. All I have to do is continue to ply it with data and when it reaches capacity . . ."

"It will offer to let you offload previous data to make room for the newer," she finished for him.

He glanced over at Neo, expecting to find her grinning as big as he was. But she had a look of near panic on her face.

"Hey. You okay?"

"No. Yeah." She looked back at her screen and started typing again. "I'm stuck on my Dr. Sevier stuff. Can't find where he went after Salt Lake City. I can't find anything."

"It doesn't matter though, right? If we don't need him to access the drive, then we don't need him at all right now. If he is a bad guy, then the cavalry will pick him up later."

But she didn't stop typing, so he didn't say anything else about it. He knew what it was to get stuck in single-track focus. This was high stress, and neither of them was working on much sleep.

Ultimately, they were going to crack the drive, and that was all that mattered. He would even take the inevitable teasing about how it had been the simplest hacking method that ended up working and how that proved he overthought everything.

Whatever. The team could tease him all he wanted. All that mattered was—

The building alarm blared.

Chapter 11

Adrenaline shot through his system at the blaring alarm. "No. Damn it, I only need a few more minutes!"

"We've got to go." Neo's voice was barely discernible over the noise. "It won't take those guards long to get down here. How much more time do you need before the drive is full and we can access it?"

He looked at the screen, then the CCTV feed on his phone. The guards were already moving. "Shit. More time than we have."

Neo started typing again. "I'm rerouting the alarm so it looks like it's coming from one of the offices on the second floor. It'll buy us a little time, but we've got to get out."

Kendrick clenched his teeth, willing the system to work faster. "I need five more minutes. Maybe ten."

Neo was packing up her computer, sliding it into the sleeve that fit in her specialized backpack. "We both know those guards will check here second. Rerouting the alarm bought us a little time but definitely not five or ten minutes' worth."

She was right. Maybe if he rerouted the data to also

come through a backdoor channel, it would speed it up enough for them to get the drive open. Ignoring the alarm, he started typing—coding as fast as he could, careful not to make a mistake. A mistake at this point would cost them everything.

He was so close. If he could just have ninety more secon—

"Fuck, they're coming down the stairs." Neo had taken his phone to watch the feed of the guards. She pulled at his arm. "We won't be able to make it to the front door we came in. They're going to have us trapped."

He didn't look at her, just kept building the code. "Forty-five more seconds."

She put her hands over his, moved her lips close to his ear—speaking low so her voice filled his head. "Kendrick, listen to me. We're going to be dead if you give this forty-five more seconds. Live to fight another day and let's get out of here in one piece."

"I can—"

"I need you to get me out of here, Blaze."

Damn it. She was right. He couldn't risk her life for this. He was cutting it too close and they were unarmed.

Neck corded, he removed his hands from the keyboard. Survival was always the most important thing.

But damn it. To have been so close . . .

She grabbed the drive and slipped it into her backpack. He closed his laptop and moved with her toward the door.

"Three guards," she said. "They're moving toward the front stairway. We can't make it to the front door."

He glanced out the door to double check it was clear. "Let's head toward the back staircase and figure something out from there. Most important thing is not getting caught in here."

They ran out the office door and toward the back of the

building, barely making it into the stairwell before the guards convened on the travel agency office.

The guards left one man in the hallway. He was watching what was going on in the office, but there was no way Kendrick and Neo could double back to the front door without being spotted.

There had to be a second door to the outside on this floor. They needed to get to that. "Let's—"

Neo popped a hand over his mouth and dragged him back under the stairs. A split second later, he heard rapid footsteps from above them, then someone talking.

"I'm in the back stairs, on my way down."

Kendrick pulled Neo into the corner under the stairs, shielding her with his body, praying the guy wouldn't check as he made it to the first floor. He could feel Neo's breath against his neck as every inch of their bodies pressed together.

God, he'd dreamed of this. But not so much with an Uzi-toting guard headed in their direction.

"Was there a sign of someone in the office?" They couldn't hear the response to the guard. "I'll head toward the back exit, see if anyone is there."

Kendrick let out a breath when the guard ran out of the stairwell without checking. But now both first-floor exit points were blocked.

He pointed up and Neo nodded. It was their only way.

As they ran, Kendrick opened his laptop again and pulled up the building blueprints. He tapped the screen. "Third floor northeast office has a utility ladder that leads up to the roof. There's a fire escape down from there."

He frowned as another set of plans caught his attention right before he closed his laptop. "That's weird. This building is built with more levels than can be seen from the street. Levels below the ground floor."

Neo pulled on his arm. "How about not dying now and saving the architecture lesson for later?"

"Yeah, let's go." They dashed the rest of the way up the stairs and down the hall toward the office they needed to break into.

She stopped at the door. "Shit. It's not an electronic lock. I can't hack it. I don't know how to get in."

"The old-fashioned way." He handed her his laptop and prayed the door was normal and not a bolt. At least it swung in. Contrary to popular television and movies, kicking in a door that swung out toward you was nearly impossible.

He lined himself up and kicked with the heel of his foot right over the doorknob. Another shoutout to the Linear guys who'd pointed out that ramming a door with his shoulder would only get him knocked back on his ass.

The door held with the first kick, but not with the second.

Neo grinned at him, handing him his laptop back. "That was as sexy as some of the stuff you do on a computer."

They both ran toward the back closet that contained the utility ladder. "If you think that's sexy, you should see me cut the grass or change a light bulb."

She let out a quiet bark of laughter. "I think you just took dirty talk to the next level."

They climbed up the metal ladder at the back of the supply closet. A second alarm started screeching as he climbed up on the top ledge and opened the half door that led out onto the roof. They ignored it since there was nothing they could do about it. He climbed up onto the roof, then reached back to help her through the small door.

"It's not going to take those guards long to get up here." He looked around for anything they could place on the door to jam it, but there was nothing.

"And it won't take geniuses to figure out we're going to

use the fire escape," she said. "All the guards have to do is wait at the bottom."

Kendrick looked around. There was only one option he could see, and it wasn't the smartest thing he'd ever suggested. "We're going to have to jump to the rooftop next door."

The leap wasn't far, but a miss would be deadly. They jogged over to the edge. There were pipes vents and large, metal utility boxes—electrical bulkheads and HVAC units— scattered along most of the side where they needed to land, but there was an opening.

They could make it. They had to. "We aim for right there so we don't impale ourselves on any pipes," he said. "We can make it. That building is a little lower, it'll help us."

She let out a shaky laugh as they backed up for a running start. "I guess now is not a great time to tell you that I don't do super well with heights?"

"Do you do better with bullets?"

"Not particularly."

He reached over and wrapped a hand around her hip and pulled her in for a fast, hard kiss. "Don't look down. Launch yourself as fast and as hard as you can. You've got a better chance of making that jump than we do against those guns coming up the ladder."

He took off her backpack as he spoke. He had at least thirty pounds of muscle on her—he would take all the extra weight.

She was staring at the ledge, face pale, lips pursed.

"Neo. Don't overthink it. Don't stop. You've got this." He kissed her again, then nudged her in the direction she needed to go. They were out of time.

He said a short prayer as she did what he'd told her to: ran and leapt.

His heart stopped, like he was in some science fiction

film where time slowed down, for the two seconds she was in the air between the buildings. But she cleared it with no problem, landing on the other side right where she needed to.

She ran toward the opposite edge. "There's another fire escape over here!"

He could hear the guards coming up the ladder. He wasn't going to make it. They'd be out the door and able to shoot him.

There was only one thing he had that could jam that door closed. His computer. It would fit perfectly under the door as a wedge.

But *fuck*. Any data he could've scraped from brute forcing the drive was going to be lost, not that there would be much of it. There was nothing on the computer that could be traced back to him, but he still hated leaving it.

But if it meant getting Neo out of here alive, it would be worth it. And they would still have the drive—that was in her backpack.

He wedged the laptop under the door. It wouldn't hold the guards for long. He could already hear them banging.

"Go! Start climbing down," he yelled at her, waving his arm in that direction. She needed to get off that roof *stat*.

He ran toward the ledge from where he was, knowing it would land him in all the industrial crap on the other rooftop. Better than shot in the back.

He took off from the roof's ledge with a powerful leap—thankful once again that being around the Linear guys had gotten him much more active than he'd been earlier in his life. He cleared the gap and landed with a hard thud, off-balance, crashing to his side atop a sharp exhaust pipe cap. He swore as he felt the metal tear his flesh.

He blew out a shuddery breath as he got to his feet. It hurt like hell, but there was no metal pipe sticking out of his body, so at least he wasn't impaled. But he could feel blood spilling onto his shirt.

He kept low as the guards yelled behind them, now on the rooftop. They'd go in the other direction toward the fire escape first, so he needed to make the most of that time.

Neo was partway down the fire escape when he got there.

"Thank God," she murmured when she saw him, then began climbing down much more quickly. He joined her in silence, ignoring the pain in his side. There was no more yelling from the guards and, thankfully, no gunshots.

Of course, the guards probably didn't want to shoot unless they had to. It would draw a lot of attention to them, and the building in general, if an automatic weapon went off from the rooftop.

"Should we hide? Wait?" Neo asked as they reached the ground in an alley.

He hunched his shoulders against the burn in his side. "No, let's not give them a chance to call in backup. We need to make it to the car while they're still figuring out what's going on."

And while he could still move with any speed. He'd get stitched up later. Right now was about surviving.

He ignored the pain, moving as quickly as he could. They crept through the streets for a couple of blocks, keeping to the shadows. But it didn't take long before he had to stop. He was bleeding pretty heavily. "Shit."

"What?" she asked, stopping also. "Do you see someone?"

He could feel his shirt torn and wet from blood. "I, uh, had a run-in with some of those pipes we were trying to avoid on the roof."

"What?" She was immediately in front of him, looking for the wound.

He knew the second she found it by the hair-singeing curse that escaped her pretty lips.

"We need to put some pressure on this wound." She slipped off her sweater, leaving her in just a tank top, and wrapped it around his waist. His breath hissed out between his teeth as she tightened and tied it. "That's not the best, but it's better than nothing."

"Aren't you going to be cold?" he asked.

"Let's worry less about me being chilly and more about you bleeding enough to leave a trail to follow."

She was right. "Roger that."

She took back her backpack with the laptop and the drive. "Where's your computer?"

"Had to use it as a doorstop to buy time with the guards. I figured the drive was the most important thing. My computer can be replaced."

"You didn't use mine to stop the guards?" Her eyes widened.

"I didn't know exactly what you'd been working on, so I didn't want to take the chance on losing something important. I didn't get far enough in the process of cracking the drive for it to make much difference." He shrugged, then winced at the pull on his waist. "Plus, mine was in my hand, not a backpack."

"I—" She shook her head and he could almost swear he saw a tear in her eye. "Thank you."

She must really like that computer. "Call it an even trade for your sweater."

She looked like she wanted to say something else, but stopped. Instead, she reached up on her toes and kissed him. Then she slipped an arm around him, taking the lead. "Let's get you home."

Chapter 12

In their former lives, Dorian and Ray had been trained by a covert government special ops group—Project Crypt—to be some of the most focused, deadliest agents on the planet.

All the Project Crypt agents had been hand selected, chosen not only for their lack of family, but for their skill sets and mental toughness, which the agency exploited. Each agent had been recruited, then trained to withstand some of the most brutal situations known to man.

To stand firm when others would crumble.

Dorian knew that it had been his early training with Project Crypt, even though they'd ended up being corrupt bastards, that had kept him alive years later when he'd been held and tortured for five weeks in a prison camp in Afghanistan.

He shouldn't be alive today, much less functioning in society, after what had happened to him in that hellhole. But because Crypt had broken all their agents down before building them back up, Dorian had found the strength inside him to survive.

He hated Project Crypt for a lot of reasons, and would've

personally hunted down any remaining members of the organization if there were any still alive. But for that one particular reason, he was thankful for them.

Ray might never have been held in an enemy prison camp, but she had gone through the same savage training as Dorian during her tenure with Project Crypt. Ray had a core of inner strength Dorian had rarely seen, and he'd worked with some of the strongest and shrewdest Special Forces soldiers in the world.

She could take down men twice her size with her bare hands. She was quick and strong, despite her petite size. She knew moves that could bring someone to their knees and have them literally begging for death.

But right now, as he and Ray stood in their kitchen, it looked like a loaf of banana bread might be her complete undoing.

The kitchen looked like a bomb had gone off. The first—and second—loaves had . . . gone wrong. He wasn't exactly sure what had happened. But when she'd hurled the contents of loaf one against the wall with enough force to rattle the windows, he'd figured . . . *gone wrong.*

Loaf two didn't get hurled but still ended up in the trash.

She was studying loaf three as it cooled on the counter with the same intensity a bomb disposal technician would consider an IED ready to blow them all to kingdom come any second.

"I just want something to take to the kids," she finally said.

He slid an arm around her waist and pulled her back against him. "I know." And he loved her for it.

"Banana bread is sweet but still a little bit healthy. So a win on both sides."

He kissed the top of her hair, so blond it was almost white. "They'll love it."

They'd been over to check on the kids every day in the three days since Lexington and his men had shown up. They hadn't talked to the kids each time, but they'd made sure they were all right.

Today, they were going to talk. The *big* talk. He and Ray had questions, and they needed answers.

If there were no adults coming to get the kids, something needed to be done. Theo and Savannah wouldn't survive in that cabin through the harsh Wyoming winter. September was fine—long days, brisk nights. Winter here was an entirely different beast.

"Let's go. I'm not going to take it."

"Those kids haven't had any baked goods in God knows how long. Bring it. We'll wrap it and take it in the backpack. It will have a chance to finish cooling while we walk."

"I don't want them to feel like they have to eat something just because I brought it. I'll leave it here."

He pulled her in for a hug. "You should think of Savannah and Theo as Eastern European versions of Jess and Ethan. Those two would let you know right away if it was bad. Theo and Savannah will also. Who knows? Maybe terrible banana bread will be the perfect icebreaker. You can feed it to Storm if need be."

That was enough to get her out the door a few minutes later, both of them moving at a gentle jog the three miles over to the hunter's shack, Storm staying right with them.

They stopped briefly to reset the small game traps by the river, looking at each other as they did it. Neither of them needed to say what they were thinking.

The kids were doing okay right now with the trapping, but they weren't experts. They wouldn't be able to catch enough to survive once the weather turned colder.

Something had to be done.

Once again, Ray approached the door while Dorian

stayed back to make sure everything was secure, and to give the children a chance to adjust, keeping Storm at his side. Only after she talked with them for a few minutes in the doorway did he come forward.

When they saw he'd brought Storm, they were even more excited. The dog stood obediently at the door as they eased closer.

"He's very friendly," Dorian assured them. "But you're smart to approach an unknown dog with caution. Good job, Theo."

The kid beamed.

"Me too," Savannah insisted. "I'm smart too."

He smiled at her even though she'd only been following the pattern her brother set for her. "Good job to you too."

Storm, used to having much louder kids than Savannah and Theo around, let them pet him, holding his head to the side so they could scratch it better. His tail wagged lazily.

Ray worked her way into the cabin and set her banana bread on the small kitchen counter. She was using the baked good to take stock of their food supplies.

They'd eaten recently, the smell of the meat that had been used in a stew still evident. That reassured him and Ray both.

"I baked some banana bread. Does anybody want some?" Ray asked.

The dog was immediately forgotten, which also spoke volumes about their level of hunger. Both he and Ray knew what it was to never quite be full, and they wouldn't wish it on anyone, particularly not two innocent kids.

Ray broke the loaf apart rather than using the knife on the counter, which was probably not very sanitary. She had her own collection of blades on her body she could've used, but that might've spooked them.

She gave large pieces of the loaf to the kids, who immediately stuffed it in their mouths. Her eyes met his over their heads. Dorian had been wrong when he'd said they were like Jess and Ethan, who would spit it out and tease her if it wasn't tasty.

Jess and Ethan, as good as they were, didn't know what it was like to go hungry. Theo and Savannah obviously did.

As soon as they'd finished the first pieces, Ray handed them second ones. They didn't wolf those quite so fast.

"Do you mind if we ask you guys some questions?" Ray asked in a bright voice that didn't really sound like hers. She was trying to keep the situation light. It worked. They nodded. Dorian gave her a nod of encouragement too.

"We noticed your accent, and it's lovely," she said with a smile. "We were trying to guess where you're from. Is it Ukraine?"

Both little heads nodded as they chewed.

"Kiev?" The capital city was a place to start. A lot of people in Ukraine lived in the cities, where the jobs were. They nodded again.

"Is it okay if I ask where your parents are?"

Little Savannah's lip began to tremble. It didn't take a genius to figure out what that meant.

"Did they die?" Dorian asked gently. There was no away around that word.

"Yes." Theo scooted closer to Savannah. "They died a few years ago in a car crash. Our neighbor Sarah took care of us."

Ray smiled. "Sarah sounds wonderful. Is she here in America too?"

More trembling lips from Savannah told them that hadn't ended well either.

"Can you tell us what happened?" Ray dropped to sit down on the ground so she was at the kids' level. "Can you tell us how you got from Kiev to here?"

Since he felt like a giant, Dorian sat on the ground too.

"When Mama and Papa died, Sarah took us in. We were sad, but then it was better. Sarah taught us English, and we were able to go to school." Theo looked over at Dorian as if he wasn't sure it was okay for a boy to like school.

"School is always good," he said simply.

Theo nodded sagely. "Sometimes Grandfather came to stay with us. He was the one who paid for school."

Their grandfather? Sarah's grandfather? Probably Sarah's if school tuition hadn't been paid for until the parents had died. Or maybe not a relative at all—maybe a friend or lover of Sarah's who had been kind to the kids?

"Where is Sarah now?" Ray asked.

Theo shook his head. "We don't know. One day she didn't come home."

How the hell had these two kids gotten all the way from Ukraine to the wilderness of Wyoming?

"Grandfather came back," Savannah added. "He stayed with us. But then the bad men came."

Dorian met Ray's eyes again. Bad men could mean many different things when defined by young children, but he didn't doubt they were telling the truth. They huddled closer together.

"Theo, buddy," he said as gently as possible, "can you tell us about the bad men?"

"They wanted Grandfather to go with them, but he said no. He wouldn't leave us."

Big tears rolled down Savannah's cheeks. Ray offered her another piece of the banana bread.

"They spoke in English because they thought I couldn't understand," Theo said. "But I could understand. And I listened even when we were supposed to be asleep."

Dorian nodded. "I don't blame you. I would've done the same." That was nothing but the truth.

Theo took a little piece of the banana bread Savannah offered and ate it before continuing. "Grandfather told the bad men if they didn't let him stay with us that he would not help them. So they went away. Grandfather spent all his time working on his computer and talking on his telephone. Those things I did not understand."

Evidently Grandfather was someone of some importance. Government official possibly? Businessman?

"And then what happened?" Ray asked.

"The men came back in a few weeks and Grandfather said that we had to go on an airplane and to bring all our clothes with us. First we drove many hours to the city called Minsk."

Dorian nodded. "That is in a country called Belarus."

Theo nodded. "We got on the airplane, and it brought us to America with Grandfather and the three bad men."

That explained them arriving on US soil. Sort of. There was definitely a great deal of information he and Ray were still missing.

"I ate a hot dog," Savannah added.

Ray ruffled her brown hair. "Hot dogs are my favorite."

Theo kept rubbing his hand on his pant leg, then glanced at Dorian. "When the bad men were not around, Grandfather told us that we must only speak English and we needed to pick American names."

"Theo and Savannah. You chose some good ones. Very American." Dorian nodded.

"Did Grandfather bring you here to the cabin?" Ray asked. "You all came to America on the airplane together, then what happened? Is he coming back for you?"

Theo and Savannah stared at each other for a long time. They were obviously trying to communicate without speaking. Make some sort of decision. Finally they nodded at each other.

"We will show you."

They got up and walked to the door. Ray and Dorian followed silently. Dorian didn't like it, and neither did Ray. She tapped on her watch so her specialized earbuds were already blocking out sounds. She'd be dependent on him to inform her if there was anything she needed to hear, but it was better than the alternative if they were walking into some sort of trap.

If so, it was elaborate and these kids should win Oscars.

He kept Storm at his side as they walked. The dog would notify them if there were unexpected visitors around. But he'd also be the first one taken out if that was the case.

Theo and Savannah held hands as they walked about five minutes from the cabin, in the opposite direction of Ray and Dorian's house. Dorian was familiar with this area of the woods from his reconnaissance—there wasn't much reason for anyone to come around here. More overgrown, more isolated.

Perfect place for a trap.

The kids stopped near a big tree, and it only took Dorian a few seconds to put it together once he looked at the foot of the tree. Ray did too. She switched off the noise-blocking aspects of her earbuds.

There was no trap here.

The ground beneath the tree had been recently disturbed in a pattern that didn't leave much question as to what it was.

A grave.

"We buried Grandfather here," Theo said.

"What happened?" Ray asked gently.

"We were supposed to get on another plane with the bad men, but Grandfather tricked them. He had a car waiting to take us away."

"They shot him with a gun," Savannah whispered. "He

was hurt bad."

"Grandfather hid us and drove us in the car. Then we came here." Theo's lips quivered.

There was so much about this story not making sense—big gaps of info missing. Dorian looked over at Ray and she shrugged. Neither of them knew whether to press for the info they wanted or to let the kids tell the story at their own pace.

"We had to walk for two days," Theo continued. "Grandfather was very weak so we carried the backpacks."

"I helped too," Savannah put in.

Dorian was trying to make sense of what the kids were saying. Who were the bad men? Who was Grandfather, and why had someone shot him? Was Grandfather on the right side or wrong side of the law?

"So you buried Grandfather here when he died?" Ray asked softly.

Theo nodded. "He died the night after we got to the cabin. Told us we were safe here, no bad men would come. We know how to hunt. We've been able to catch rabbits. We will stay here like Grandfather wanted."

Savannah slipped her hand into Theo's as he said the words. Obviously, they had talked about this.

These kids were survivors. Dorian recognized the same trait he shared with Ray. A refusal to roll over just because things looked bleak.

Dorian walked over to Theo and placed his hand on the boy's shoulder, touching him for the first time. "You've done good work here. Done what you needed to do. That's impressive."

Keeping his sister alive and fed. Burying the dead. Focusing on the here and now rather than panicking. It wasn't easy for grown-ass adults, much less an eleven-year-old kid.

Theo nodded.

"Let's go back and eat the rest of the banana bread," Ray said. "Tomorrow, maybe I can bring you some more."

They turned and walked back toward the cabin. Dorian watched as Savannah slipped her little hand into Ray's. Ray, who could barely stand to be touched, gripped it tightly.

As soon as they were back at the cabin, Dorian excused himself, leaving Storm with them, while Ray sat down with the kids to read the children's books.

Their appearance at this cabin hadn't been happenstance. It had been a well-thought-out plan. *Grandfather's* plan. He'd known they'd be isolated for a while, so had brought traps, books, and clothing for weeks.

He'd had a plan, but it definitely hadn't included him dying.

But why here? Of all the places he might've hidden with two children in the United States, how the hell had they ended up in the wilderness of Wyoming?

Dorian slipped deeper into the woods, caught two more rabbits, and took them back to the cabin. He would've liked to have gotten more, but there was no refrigeration, so it would have been a waste. But at least tonight and tomorrow, the kids would not be hungry.

As he approached the shack, Ray and the kids were laughing, reading the books again, Ray correcting their English when they got it wrong.

What the hell were they going to do about these kids? They couldn't stay here. Their independence and gumption would be no match for the Wyoming winter.

Theo and Savannah needed a family, foster care of some type.

He and Ray were going to have to report them. It was for the best.

Chapter 13

"Honey, are you sure? I don't like the thought of leaving you here for an evening shift alone. And this is supposed to be your day off to work on your little art project."

Little art project.

Wavy Bollinger forced a smile at the older woman she'd been working with here at the Frontier Diner for ten years and had known her entire life. Leeann didn't mean any harm. "Little" was her preferred adjective for almost everything. She referred to Linear Tactical as that "little business" the boys had built.

Still, it made Wavy's teeth grind to hear her passion referred to as such.

She kept the smile plastered on her face. "No problem, Leeann. You know Mr. Earl wouldn't call you if he wasn't feeling poorly."

The older woman's face crumpled. "Since his stroke . . ."

Wavy reached out and squeezed her hand. "Absolutely. You go on home to him. And I'm not here alone. Nolan's here, and Matthew. So you don't need to worry."

Granted, neither the cook nor the dishwasher would

come out here to the front of the house unless Wavy started screaming her head off. But at least they would come.

Leeann was a little on edge since some bad guys had followed Wyatt Highfield back into the area a few days ago and might still be hanging around. Since the Frontier was in the middle of town, the Linear guys had asked Wavy to keep an eye out for anyone suspicious. Something about an organization known as Mosaic and that people had been killed because of it.

Leeann had overheard the request and had been a mess ever since, even though there hadn't been any sign of anything out of the ordinary. Thank God she hadn't heard that Mosaic was a human trafficking network or Leeann probably would've joined her husband with the stroke. The older woman worried.

The good thing about a town the size of Oak Creek was that people looked out for one another. That's why Wavy loved living here.

The bad thing about a town the size of Oak Creek was that, good Lord have mercy, people were always up in your business. That's why the town usually drove her crazy.

It was time for her to get out. She'd been feeling that way more and more. But a lifetime's worth of ties to one place weren't easy to unravel.

Wavy sent Leeann on her way. She'd been looking forward to spending the evening painting, but her art would wait. It had been waiting a decade for her to actually do something with it.

The evening went like most any given weeknight at the diner. Leeann had gotten them through the dinner rush so now it was only a few stragglers for the couple hours until they closed. Some teenagers sitting at separate booths but flirting back and forth. Old Mr. Collier who was a regular on any given night when he was missing his wife of sixty-seven years who'd died a few months ago. He sat at the counter with his magazine, just liking to be around other people. A young family who'd decided to splurge and go out for pie.

And then the man who walked in fifteen minutes before closing.

Everything about him had Wavy on high alert. She'd been around the Linear Tactical guys long enough to recognize when someone was at a place for more than merely pie.

She couldn't see the color of his eyes, but she recognized fierceness in his gaze. Strong chin and carved jaw. Broad shoulders, trim waist. A warrior's awareness.

Everything about this man screamed danger.

"Can I get you something?" He had chosen the very back booth and had his back to the wall so he could see the whole restaurant. The same booth the Linear guys tended to gravitate toward.

The man glanced at her but she had no doubt he was fully aware of everything that was happening in the diner. Brown eyes, she could see them now, with little specks of gold. "Just coffee. Thanks."

She nodded and walked to get it. He was probably stopping for coffee before a long road trip or something. No need to assume the worst just because he sat in the back booth and was aware of what was going on around him.

She made a fresh pot before bringing a steaming mug over to him. She wasn't normally so suspicious. The Linear guys might have criminals following them everywhere, but Wavy did not want to be someone who refused to trust others for no reason.

She smiled at him as she set down the coffee. "You need creamer?" She should've asked that when she first took the order but she'd been too busy assuming he was about to kill everyone in the place.

"No, black is fine."

Of course it was. How could someone who had a jaw that chiseled drink anything but black coffee?

She wanted to paint him. She didn't normally like to create anything having to do with people, but she'd love to paint this man.

Naked.

No! No, not naked. Just regular.

Or . . . half-naked. Which half?

"Are you okay?" He was looking at her with one dark eyebrow raised.

And why wouldn't he be? She was staring at him like some sort of pervy-perv. "Um, yeah. Sorry, I'm fine. I—"

His phone lit up on the table, a text message coming in. She couldn't read the whole thing, but one word very definitely caught her attention.

Mosaic.

All thoughts of painting him flew from her mind. He slid the phone toward him so she couldn't read the message anymore.

"I'll-I'll just be over here if you need anything else."

"Thanks."

She walked toward Mr. Collier as Dangerous Man's phone chirped behind her. She couldn't hear most of his conversation, but one word caught her attention once again.

Kendrick.

Oh shit.

"You know what, Mr. Collier? Your meal is on us tonight." She smiled at the older man. "We're glad you came in. It's good to see you."

"Why, thank you, Wavy . . ."

"Excuse me for a minute, I just need to take care of something in the back. I'll see you next time."

She hoped Mr. Collier would leave. She didn't want him around if things with Dangerous Man turned ugly.

She took out her phone and texted her brother Finn.

Stranger just came in diner. Suspicious. He got a text with word Mosaic, *talked to someone about Kendrick.*

Finn's response was almost immediate.

Get out.

She peeked out the kitchen window. The guy was still sitting in the booth. If they could get information from him, maybe it would help put these Mosaic criminal people behind bars. Human traffickers were the scum of the earth, and Wavy wanted to do her part to take them down.

She looked over at Nolan, but the cook had his headphones on. She didn't want to involve him if she didn't have to. In a physical altercation, Dangerous Man would win. Nolan would be no match. Neither would Matthew, the teenage dishwasher.

She'd have to keep the guy here herself.

She shot off another text to Finn.

I'll keep him here, you send someone.

Response was immediate again. *No. Get out.*

Damn it, she was going to do her part. *You better hurry.*

She slipped her phone back in her apron pocket, ignoring it when it started buzzing a few seconds later, Finn calling rather than texting.

The guy looked like he was fishing for his wallet so she loaded a tray full of slices of the diner's different pies and walked it over to him.

"Hi. I know you said you just wanted coffee but we're about to close, and I've still got all these pies. I hate for them to go to waste; we'll just have to throw them out." Her brothers would have a heart attack if she ever once threw away extra pie from the Frontier. "Can I offer you a slice for free?"

The guy was going to turn her down. She could already see it.

She tripped and dumped the tray in his lap.

"Oh my God! I'm so clumsy, I'm so sorry." She set down her tray and immediately started wiping huge chunks of pie flowing all down his front. Chocolate smeared into apple, and lemon meringue covered it all.

But it kept him in the booth. So she kept wiping.

Oh God, had she just brushed his crotch? Now her mortification wasn't acting.

He grabbed her hands, more gently than she would've expected given the current circumstances. "I've got it." He set her away from him. "You have a bathroom?"

She pointed to the hall near the back corner. He stood and began walking in that direction.

Finn better hurry up. Short of undressing the guy, she was probably out of ways to keep him here.

Dangerous Man's phone rang again right as he got to the hallway of the bathroom.

"Where the hell are you? I'm going to put a fucking cap in your ass myself. This town is already on my last nerve."

Oh shit. Maybe she should've gotten out when Finn told her to.

She pretended to wipe down the table so she could watch him go into the bathroom. She needed to call in backup while he was in there.

But instead of going in the bathroom, he went through the door that led out to the side alley outside.

Damn it. That was where some of the customers went when they needed a smoke. It didn't really lead anywhere, but you could get out if you wound around the side and went through the back.

He was going to get away if she didn't stop him.

Knowing she was all sorts of stupid, especially since he'd just threatened to pop a cap in someone's ass, she still ran for the side employee door. She would cut him off and crack him on the head with her tray. He wouldn't be expecting anyone coming at him from the opposite direction.

She hoped.

It wasn't the best of plans, but she didn't have time to develop a full-fledged Linear Tactical mission. All she needed was to buy a few more minutes until Finn arrived. If this was her chance to stop human traffickers, then she was about to get all ninja with this tray.

She rushed toward the back door through the kitchen. Nolan saw her, but she didn't have time to explain.

Out the back she could hear the guy saying something else on the phone about taking whatever opportunity presented itself. He ended the call, and she could hear him muttering about *fucking pie*.

He was getting closer.

She backed herself against the darkened wall, waiting for him to come around the corner. When he did, she brought her tray down on the side of his head as hard as she could.

He let out a roar. "Mother fuc—"

She moved backward, then brought the tray back up to hit him again, was swinging back down when someone caught it from the side.

"Sorry, lady, I can't let you beat up my boss, even if he did threaten to put a cap in my ass. Seriously, who says that?"

Wavy waited for some sort of blow or to be shoved to the ground, but it didn't happen.

Maybe now would be a good time to do the screaming-her-head-off thing. Hope Nolan and Matthew could hear her.

Dangerous Man turned to her. "What the hell is wrong with you, lady?"

"I don't like human traffickers. That's what's wrong with me."

"What are you talking about?" The guy was covered in pie and rubbing the side of his head, glaring at her. Now she really expected some sort of violence.

"I'm gonna have to ask you to step away from my sister."

Baby. Thank God.

Her brother walked farther into the back alley, the moon gleaming off the gun he was pointing at them. Dangerous Man and the other guy both backed up, holding their hands up near their heads.

"Your sister has assaulted me with both pie and her tray in the past three minutes."

"Yeah, she's sassy like that," Baby said. "And although she and I are going to have words about her wasting pie like that, I'm still going to need you to step farther away from her."

Baby stepped into the light, and both men took another step back.

"Look, I think there is some mistake here," said the man who'd stopped her from getting her second thwack in. "We don't mean any harm."

Dangerous Man glared at her and muttered something suspiciously like, "Speak for yourself."

"Wavy doesn't generally attack her customers without due cause," Baby said. "Bad for tips."

"This guy was talking about Mosaic and Kendrick. That was enough for me to let Finn know there was trouble."

"And Finn told you to attack him?" Baby raised an eyebrow. "Using *pie*?"

Wavy shrugged. "More or less."

"Can I join the party back here?" Zac Mackay came through the same entrance Wavy had used. "Finn called. Asked me to stop by since I was already in town."

His voice was slightly breathless. Zac may be acting cool, but he'd been in a rush to get here.

"Wavy might have caught a couple of members of Mosaic," Baby said.

"Oh for fuck's sake," Dangerous man said. "I'm not—"

Wavy held up the tray like she was going to hit him again. He rolled his eyes and turned to Zac. "You going to tell them or just let me be assaulted by Killer Waitress here?"

Zac chuckled and Wavy grimaced. That wasn't good.

"Waverly, Baby, can I introduce Ian DeRose? He owns Zodiac Tactical. We work with them occasionally. He is also the foremost expert on Mosaic and how to stop them."

Ian DeRose. Shit. She'd heard the guys talk about him and Zodiac before.

Baby lowered his weapon, laughing. "Sorry, man. I got a panicked call that Waverly here had a possible tango, and that I needed to get my ass over to help, stat."

"Thanks for checking your info before shooting," Ian said. He raised an eyebrow at her, message clear: she hadn't checked.

Boo-hoo. She hadn't had a real weapon either.

"This is Landon Black, my right hand," Ian said. "We got a message from Kendrick that he might have an update. He's not at his place."

Zac nodded. "Yeah, I can help you with that. He's at a safe house."

"I'm getting back home to my fiancée. I'll let Finn know to stand down." Baby reached in to hug her and whispered in her ear, "Way to take down the enemy, sis."

"Piss off." But she kissed his cheek.

He laughed as he walked away.

"I'm going to grab a slice of pie." Zac glanced at Ian's shirt and pants. "If there's any left."

"I'll take some of that action," Landon said. "I've already heard about the pie here."

That left Wavy and Ian *Dangerous Man* DeRose out here alone.

"I guess I owe you an apology." Why was that so hard to say? With anyone else she would've already apologized while laughing at how she'd been such a moron. Make a joke about free pie for life.

But somehow, she was too aware of Ian DeRose to laugh like she did with everyone else. Instead, she had this unnerving need to run away from him—or step closer.

"You were trying to detain a member of Mosaic, so that justifies a lot." He looked at her with brown eyes that were way too intense. Like he never let his guard down.

She felt the uncanny need to reach up and rub her fingers in the dark hair behind his ear. A touch to soothe. To connect.

She had no idea why. He didn't seem like he would accept that sort of touch from anyone, much less a stranger.

"Still, bad guy or not, I'm sorry I hit you."

He took a step closer, and she couldn't help but take a step back. His smile turned the slightest bit predatory as he moved toward her again.

Her back was to the wall. Literally and figuratively.

He got closer.

He reached down and she thought he was going to touch her, but he grabbed the tray in her hand instead.

"Next time, come at your enemy's temple with the edge of the tray where it's hardest." He tapped the edge with his knuckles. "You're a lot more likely to do damage that way, Wavy Bollinger."

And then he was gone.

Chapter 14

Kendrick was hurt. He was trying to play it off as if it were just a scratch, but he'd been leaning on Neo more heavily with every step as they made their way toward the car. Thank God they hadn't run into any of the armed guards. If Kendrick had to run, they'd be up shit creek.

He'd jumped into that section of the roof to make sure he didn't draw any attention, or the guards' guns, in her direction.

He'd taken his own computer and stuffed it under that door to buy them more time.

And *she'd* been the one who triggered the alarm in the first place.

He'd been getting too close to cracking that drive, and she'd panicked. She'd thought she could trigger the alarm, then reroute the guards to give her and Kendrick time to make it out the front door. But the guards had moved too fast, and Kendrick had moved too slow, spending every last second he could to try to get that intel.

And now, he was bleeding all over her sweater as she got them into the car and started back toward the safe house.

"Maybe we should take you to the hospital."

"I'll be okay. Let's get back, and I'll call Anne. She's patched everyone up over the past couple of years. Plus, she makes sure all of us are up to date on our tetanus shot."

"Are you sure? It's not a gunshot, so they're not going to report it to the authorities."

He grabbed her hand, giving it a squeeze, which just made her feel worse. "I promise, I'll be fine. It needs to be cleaned and probably a couple of stitches, but that's all. Plus, I have a hunch I want to check out."

"About the drive?"

"Peripherally. It's actually about that entire building. I think there might be a secret sublevel. Not just a basement, something more. It would certainly explain the Terminator security."

She didn't say anything. Letting him concentrate on the building was probably the best thing she could do.

How much longer was she going to be able to hold him off from the drive? She'd gotten lucky using the Trojan horse to block him from accessing it earlier, and he'd almost cracked it anyway.

It wasn't going to take much longer for him to realize there was no brilliant new player in the game. There was merely one he trusted who was using his own talents against him.

She glanced over at his waist. Now that they weren't in constant motion, his wound didn't seem to be gushing blood. She still wished he would let her take him to a hospital.

She didn't even bother parking down the street when they arrived back at the safe house. If they needed to get out quickly, she wanted to have the car nearby.

She walked around the car to help him, but he'd already gotten out by himself, brain focused on the task at hand.

"Can I borrow your laptop to see if my thinking about

the schematics is correct?" he asked as she unlocked the door.

She gritted her teeth. "First we're going to take care of that cut."

He let out a sigh. "Yes, ma'am."

He leaned against the kitchen counter as she untied her ruined sweater, then eased his shirt away from the wound. The puncture didn't look too deep, but it definitely needed to be cleaned and stitched. "That looks painful. You definitely could use a few stitches."

He craned out his neck so he could see it without stretching too much. "I'm sure there's some sort of med kit in here somewhere. Let's see if there's some butterfly bandages. I'll call Dr. Anne in a couple hours, and we can see what she thinks. After we look into that building closer."

They both jumped at the knock on the front door. Kendrick reached into one of the drawers and pulled out a gun. He used the other arm to wrap around her and pull her behind him.

She grabbed a knife from the set on the counter. It wouldn't help if it was the guards with Uzis, but she wasn't going to hide behind Kendrick like some cowardly damsel in distress.

"Do you think we were followed?" she asked. "I kept an eye out and didn't see anyone."

He shook his head. "If one of those guards had followed us, I don't think they'd be knocking."

His phone chimed on the counter. She reached around him and picked it up. "It says, 'You've been a naughty boy, Blaze. It's Ian. Let me in.' "

She could feel the tension flow out of him, and he put the gun back in the drawer.

"Ian DeRose?" she asked.

He nodded, then walked toward the door. "I didn't think he would get here for a few more hours."

Kendrick checked the monitor panel on the counter that showed the camera feed to the front door just to be certain, then walked over and opened it. Two men walked inside, one with darker hair and an olive-toned complexion, the other a little more blond.

Both looked just as focused and dangerous as any of the Linear Tactical guys, immediately taking in the room, scanning for potential threats probably without even realizing it. Kendrick shut and locked the door behind them.

"What happened, Blaze?" the darker one said, pointing at Kendrick's wound. "Girlfriend get tired of your mouth, decide to show you who's boss?"

Kendrick smiled. "Ian, Landon, this is Neo LeBarre. She's helping me crack the drive. Neo, Ian DeRose is the owner and general mastermind behind Zodiac Tactical, and Landon Black is one of his top employees."

Landon smiled. "Someone has to help keep up Ian's *general mastermind* appearance. It's a fulltime job."

As she shook their hands, she recognized the warrior in both of them, despite their smiles and friendliness.

Ian was a little older and definitely the darker and more watchful of the two—his brown eyes piercing, cold. Landon seemed more laid back, but still probably equally dangerous. More like a panther at ease but capable of turning deadly at any moment.

Both of these men had killed and would do so again if needed. She could feel it in her bones. And like it or not, she was pitted against them.

She forced a smile. "It's nice to meet you. We were about to see if we could find the first-aid kit and patch up boy genius. That'll be the last time he gives me lip."

Everyone laughed. Good. Laughing was better than being suspicious of her.

"Mind if I use my field medic training again and take a closer look?" Landon asked. "I can already tell you with just a glance that needs a few stitches."

"Sure." Kendrick was studying Ian. "If you tell me why DeRose has lemon pie in his hair."

Ian let out something that resembled a growl. "I met Wavy Bollinger."

That was it, nothing else. She and Kendrick looked over at Landon for more info.

He laughed. "We were looking for you a few hours ago. Wavy mistook Ian for a member of Mosaic, knocked him upside the head. Pie was sacrificed. Collateral damage."

"I might need a moment of silence," Kendrick muttered.

"For me, I hope," Ian said. "Not the fucking pie."

"You've never had the pie," she and Kendrick said at the same time.

She met his eyes, a smile on both their faces. Then hers faded.

He's hurt because of you.

In the end, she sat and watched as Kendrick perched on a stool, his arm up and hand wrapped around his dark head, as Landon ended up giving him six stitches. The lidocaine they'd found in the med kit took the edge off, but she winced every time Kendrick flinched as the needle pierced his skin.

He did that to protect you. He has that wound because you sounded the alarm.

This had gone further than she'd ever planned it to. If that wound had been a little deeper or closer to his stomach, he could be dead.

While Landon stitched him up, Kendrick got them up to date on the status of the drive. He explained about Dr.

Sevier and Hemingway Travel Agency and why he felt the building was also key to finding out more about Mosaic.

When Landon was done and putting away the medical supplies, she handed Kendrick the shirt she'd gotten from the bedroom. He slipped it on but didn't button it up. The white bandage over his dark skin was a jarring reminder of her deceit.

She turned to look at Ian. "I don't really understand your tie to Mosaic. Are you law enforcement or something?"

The big man shrugged. "Zodiac does work with law enforcement on occasions. But mostly, we're private sector."

"I don't really understand what Mosaic is. I've dipped my fingers in a lot of questionable pools during my hacker years, and the name has never come up."

"That's because they don't exist anymore." Landon zipped up the first-aid kit.

Kendrick rolled his eyes. "You stitching me up for the past thirty minutes tells me otherwise."

Neo pushed her hair back from her shoulders. "I guess I don't understand why we're not working with law enforcement." Not that she wanted to bring cops in on this. The situation was fraught enough as it was.

Ian leaned against the kitchen counter and crossed his arms over his chest. "Five years ago, I was part of an undercover group put together specifically to take down Mosaic."

"With, like, the FBI or something?" she asked.

"Or something." Ian nodded. "It was a multi-agency task force called Omega Sector. A best-of-the-best sort of thing."

She refrained from rolling her eyes. "Omega Sector? Best-of-the-best?"

"Believe me, I've mentioned the eighties movie references myself." Ian gave a half smile.

"So they sent you undercover? As what?"

"Basically, as myself. New billionaire with underground

connections and no known loyalties. At least, that's what I looked like on the surface."

"I'm assuming since we're dealing with Mosaic again today that your undercover mission wasn't very successful?"

"Actually, the mission was considered a success. We shut them down. At that time, Mosaic was into weapon, information, and technology sales. Selling power to people who were willing to pay for it."

Ian ran a hand through his dark hair. "I got the information we needed to take down Mosaic's leader and end it for good. But I . . ."

He trailed off. She waited for him to continue, but he didn't. He was staring at some point on the floor, trapped in a hell none of them could see but all of them could feel.

"Ian was able to take down Mosaic, but there was a price." Landon walked by and slapped his friend on the shoulder. The touch was enough to bring Ian back into the present.

If whatever had happened was enough to put nightmares into the eyes of a man as tough as Ian DeRose, it had been a damned high price indeed.

"I'm sorry," she whispered. She slid a little closer to Kendrick; she couldn't help it.

Ian nodded. "Mosaic was disbanded—a shit ton of arrests. We thought it was gone for good. But then about six months ago, I started receiving messages that suggested Mosaic was somehow back in play."

"What sort of messages?" Kendrick asked.

Ian and Landon glanced at each other. "I was sent some video footage of one of my Zodiac agents, Aspen Roarke. She was supposed to be on a long-term mission in Marrakesh but she'd been taken."

"The footage showed Aspen doing things she would never do of her own free will," Landon added.

Ian pushed away from the counter. "What she was doing wasn't important. What's important is whoever sent it made sure we knew that they were controlling her, and that Mosaic 2.0 was in business. And that they'd also branched out into new territory—human trafficking via artificial intelligence."

Kendrick shot Neo a look. "That would explain why they've brought in a neuromorphic engineer."

Ian nodded. "Claude Sevier."

"You know him?" Kendrick asked.

"He reached out to me a few months ago. At the time, I wasn't sure who he was and thought he might be part of a trap."

"He's the one who created the drive." Kendrick leaned back against the counter. "If you can get ahold of him, this thing would be a hell of a lot easier to crack."

"I haven't heard from him in more than a month. He's not working for Mosaic; he's trying to stop them. But he's also aware that they're going to kill him if they find out what he's doing. I've got a team in Paris looking for him."

"He's not in Paris anymore." Neo wanted to pull at her hair.

God, this all kept getting worse. Dr. Sevier was a *good* guy. At least when it looked like he was working for Mosaic, she could justify giving info about him to Varela. But to know Sevier was trying to *stop* this Mosaic? "He flew into Salt Lake City three weeks ago. Was supposed to go to Los Angeles, but there's no official record of him anywhere once he landed."

Landon nodded. "I'll get someone out to that area right away. Let me call the office." He handed Ian a file as he walked into the other room.

Ian held it out toward them. "This file is a printout of the data we've been able to obtain—either from intel we've collected ourselves or from what's been sent as taunts."

"Anything helpful?" Kendrick took it and sat down at the table.

"Only in terms of lighting fires under our asses to get Mosaic shut down. It's not pretty."

"Shit," Kendrick muttered under his breath. He thumbed through the photos in the file. "Oh Jesus."

Ian scrubbed his hand over his face. "Yeah. Hope you don't have delicate stomachs. Evidently, Mosaic now likes to cage their victims while they 'train' them."

Chapter 15

"Ian, man, I'm so sorry we haven't made more progress on the drive. It's been a nightmare. I've been way too cocky or something, but this thing has been an absolute fucking nemesis."

Neo stared down at the pictures spread out over the table as Kendrick continued to apologize for something that wasn't his fault. Ian and Landon assured him that they knew he was doing his best. That this new version of Mosaic was more well organized and technically savvy than the first group ever had been.

Sevier had been trying to use Mosaic's own system against them, but something had evidently gone wrong.

The discussion went on around her at a distance, like it was on the other side of some sort of thick bubble, and she could only hear if she forced herself to concentrate.

And she couldn't force herself to concentrate on it anymore. Not after seeing these pictures.

She was backing away emotionally from the present—zipping herself into her own skin, removed from everyone.

She could separate herself enough from it all to recognize her behavior for what it was: a coping mechanism.

She'd developed it as a child when she'd been bounced from one foster home to another. There came a point—and most chronic foster kids learned to pinpoint it—when she'd known each time that a decision had been made and she was no longer going to be part of the inner circle. Her only option had been to wrap walls around herself so no pain could get through.

As a child, she hadn't had the choice of whether to stay or go. The choice to be removed from each family had been made whether she wanted it or not.

But this time, she was making the choice to take herself out of the inner circle.

She ran her fingers along the photo of one of the caged women Ian had shown them. A teenager. Her eyes were blank, haunted.

Hopeless.

Every time Neo stopped Kendrick from making forward progress on the drive, she was contributing to whatever physical or emotional torture the people trapped by Mosaic were going through.

It was time to take herself out of the equation. It was the only way. If she didn't, Varela would certainly go through with his threat to tell Kendrick and everyone else at Linear what she'd done, about the surveillance she'd set up. That, coupled with how she'd hindered things here, would remove her from the equation anyway.

Unlike the child she'd been, who'd had no choice in whether she was shown the door, she could at least make the choice now. It was better for everyone if she just walked, didn't let them know how much she'd betrayed their trust. Better for everyone if she just disappeared.

But walking away from the people she'd surrounded

herself with for the past year—the closest thing she'd ever had to a permanent family—was going to hurt. Her subconscious was trying to protect her, withdrawing until the wall was solid, until nothing could hurt her.

"Hey." She flinched as Kendrick trailed a gentle hand across her shoulder. "You okay?"

She'd have to leave him behind. She rubbed the heel of her hand over her chest where the wall cracked at the thought of never seeing him again. Agony bubbled through the fissure.

"I know it's hard to see right now, but we're going to get these bastards." He wrapped an arm around her, pulling her up from the table and against his chest.

She had no right to be here. No right to take any comfort from him in any way. But she couldn't seem to stop herself. She breathed in his scent and snuggled closer. If these were her last few minutes with him, she wanted to spend them being close.

The sun was coming up as Ian and Landon said their goodbyes. Ian was going to look into the Hemingway building further and see what he could dig up.

She watched, arms wrapped around herself, as Kendrick made some sort of joke as he walked the guys to the door. They chuckled and clapped him on the shoulder.

He was still his same charming, positive self despite their recent adversity. Despite being wounded. Despite being frustrated, exhausted, and in pain.

Kendrick was a force of nature. And damned if his confidence and contagious smile hadn't reeled her in from day one.

How was she supposed to leave him? This charming, sexy, brilliant man who was not only her equal, but her *balance*.

She loved him.

They'd done nothing more than kiss a few times. Hadn't even been on a date. But she still knew it was true. She loved Kendrick. It had happened so gradually and gently, hidden behind jokes and friendship and banter, that she couldn't even say when she'd fallen for him.

But she had. He'd made it easy. It was his way.

Coming to terms with the knowledge that she loved him wasn't difficult. Knowing she had to leave him behind was much harder. She wrapped her arms more tightly around herself like it would help keep the pieces of her shattered heart inside her body.

He turned and faced her once Landon and Ian were gone. The corner of his lips pulled down into a frown. She forced herself to lower her arms to her side. Forced herself to not fold under the weight of the pain she knew would be crushing her the minute she walked out the door.

"Hey. Doing okay?" He took a couple steps closer. "I know those pictures are hard to look at."

Even harder when you are the one actively helping it.

But not for long. She could give him that.

"Yeah. Hard."

He leaned back against the counter. "Want to get a couple hours of sleep before we get cracking at it again? Give our brains a chance to reboot?"

She walked toward him. "How are you feeling?"

"Oh, you know, about the usual for someone who took a leap off the top of a building, got stabbed by scrap metal, then stitched up by a former Navy SEAL." He winked at her.

She kissed him. She knew he wasn't expecting it. Hell, *she* wasn't expecting it. But she couldn't stop herself. She was about to walk out of here and leave him forever. She was already a selfish bitch. Might as well take one more thing for herself.

The kiss lacked all finesse and romance. She hooked one arm around his neck, pulled him down to her, and kissed him. Like he was the air she needed to survive.

It only took him a few seconds to recover from his surprise and take control. His hands slid into her hair and tilted her head so he had better access to her mouth.

They should have had weeks of slow, soft kisses. There should've been dates and flirting and teasing and getting to first base and second base . . .

There would be none of that now. All that was left was this jumbled mess inside made up of tragedy and heartbreak and . . . *want.*

She cursed herself for all the months that she'd wanted him but had held him at bay. And now all she had was this moment. It was all she would ever get.

Her lips consumed his, her fingers trailing up his chest, over his shoulders, feeling the shape of his neck, his ears, his head—willing her memory to engrain every feeling, every touch, into her very consciousness.

She breathed in every bit of him that she could, trying to store it away for all the time she had ahead of her when he wouldn't be there.

She pushed up against him, breasts aching as they crushed against his chest. Some distant part of her told her he was wounded, she should be careful, but her movements didn't seem to bother him. His hand slid out of her hair and down her back, reaching to cup her ass and pull her harder against him.

They both groaned.

But then he wrenched away from her. "Goddamn, Neo." He was breathing as hard as she was.

"What? Did I hurt you? This isn't what you want?" *You realized I've been betraying you not only the past couple of days but basically since you've known me?*

"Hell yes, it's what I want. I'm about to combust here. But . . ." He ran his hands up her hips along her waist, up over her back and shoulders until they were threaded in her hair again. He bent his head until his forehead rested against hers. "Are you okay? Believe me when I say, yes, I definitely want this. But it doesn't have to be right now. We have time. I can wait."

She swallowed the hysterical giggle that threatened to rupture out of her. *Time.* Of course he would think they had time. Why wouldn't he?

She sucked in a shuddery breath. "If you feel up to it, then I want you now. I don't want to wait. If today has taught me anything, it's that none of us are guaranteed tomorrow."

That, at least, was true.

But maybe it was better if they didn't. Maybe, after everything was said and done, when she was gone and he'd figured out the depth to which she'd betrayed him, he'd be glad they hadn't had sex.

She closed her eyes and forced herself to take a step back. "You know what? You're right, let's not—"

She never finished the sentence. He moved with a dizzying speed, especially for someone injured. His hands were back down on her ass again, lifting her so she was pressed against him exactly where she most wanted to be before he spun her and set her on the counter. Her legs automatically hooked around his hips, crossing behind him, bringing them closer. If his injury bothered him, he wasn't showing it at all.

"You feel that." His fingers bit into her ass with almost bruising force as he thrust against her. The motion left no question whatsoever about whether he wanted her or not.

"That." He thrust again. "Has been a near constant in my life since the moment you walked into it. So believe me when I say you *never* have to ask me if this is what I want. It is."

"Okay then, Blaze." She met his eyes. "Let's burn."

The smile he gave her was so wickedly decadent that she couldn't help but rub herself against him. When his lips found her neck and bit with just enough force to make her gasp, he whispered in her ear, "I want to spend a long time figuring out what makes you squirm and sigh and moan, Neoma."

His words were making her do all three.

He kept her pinned as he worked his way along her jaw and neck with nipping little kisses. He only let her go long enough to pull her tank top over her head.

The sheer male appreciation in his eyes as he unhooked her bra and ran his fingers over her naked breasts was a huge blast against the wall she was trying to keep around her emotions. She felt the crack, knew she couldn't withstand another direct hit without her walls crumbling entirely.

That couldn't happen.

If her walls fell, she'd tell him what she'd done and beg his forgiveness. He'd walk away from her. She wasn't sure she'd survive it.

"Take me to bed, Kendrick. I don't want soft touches and pretty words. I want you to fuck me deep and hard.

His eyes narrowed for a second as he studied her, as if he knew he should press the issue behind her crude words, but he also had a half-naked woman in front of him.

Asking him to fuck her deep and hard.

Deep and hard won out. His lips crashed back into hers, and she could feel the desperation in the kiss. The need. Recognized it because the same desire was coursing through her veins.

She pushed against his chest so she could slide down off the counter. "I want you in the bed. And I'm not calling

Landon back to stitch you up again, so you're not going to carry me."

She grabbed the top of his jeans and towed him to the bedroom as she walked backward. Their mouths stayed fused together as they moved, like neither of them could stand to be even an inch apart. She knew why she wanted him close—she didn't want to waste a single second of the few they had left together.

She had no idea what would have him feeling the same way, but she would take it.

They kicked off their shoes and were both fishing for each other's buttons on their jeans by the time they made it to the bedroom.

"Protection," he muttered against her mouth.

She shimmied her jeans the rest of the way off as he walked into the connected bathroom. When he walked back out, naked, she sucked in her breath at the glorious sight of him.

He grinned. "See something you like?"

God, this man with all his cocky charm. How was she ever supposed to live without him? She could feel her face fall—he'd struck another blow to her defenses just by being himself.

He rushed toward the bed. "Whoa. Hey, I'm sorry. I was kidding. I didn't mean . . ." He laughed awkwardly.

How many more times and in how many different ways was she going to tear at his confidence when the truth was, he was damned near perfect?

She crawled to the edge of the bed and rose up on her knees so she could run her nails across his chest. "I do see something I like. And you sure as hell don't look like some computer nerd. So please tell me you found the protection we need."

He held up the condom packet.

"Then please get your fine, Blasian ass in this bed."

He reached out a hand and tucked a strand of hair behind her ear. "You sure you don't want to tell me what's going on?"

She almost did.

For a second, she almost took a chance and told him everything. There was never going to be someone as attuned to her as Kendrick. Maybe if she explained from the beginning he'd give her a second chance.

Those brown eyes stared at her as if this was some natural part of sex—waiting for her to get her shit together.

She couldn't do it. Couldn't tell him. Couldn't watch disappointment cloud that handsome face. It was better to walk away from him entirely than watch him pull away from her knowing she couldn't be trusted.

So she shot him a sexy grin of her own and tamped down everything she was hiding from him.

She reached out and grabbed the condom from his hand and ripped open the package. Then she stroked her fingers up and down his hard length before wrapping her fist around him.

The groan that fell from his throat was all the encouragement she needed. She teased him a little more before sliding the condom in place. Then kissed along his jaw up to his ear.

"Hard. Fast. Deep."

Chapter 16

This woman, with her clever fingers all over him and her dirty words in his ear, was going to be the death of him.

But despite the pleasure threatening to make this entire rendezvous embarrassingly short, Kendrick couldn't help but realize there was something going on in that brilliant mind of hers that she wasn't telling him.

And he had no idea what it was.

Of course, there were plenty of reasons for her brain to be freaking out. They'd broken into a building, leapt from a rooftop over what would've been certain death if they'd miscalculated. She'd dragged his bleeding carcass through alleys to get them back here.

Then they'd spent the past three hours listening to and seeing the horrors of Mosaic, knowing they could stop it if they just figured out *how*.

Yeah, that could be a lot for a brain to process. Hell, it was a lot for *his* brain to process.

But God, every kiss from Neo felt laced with desperation, from the moment they'd started in the kitchen. Like she was holding on to him as her lifeline. He didn't understand why or what was going on.

But when was that ever *not* the case with Neo?

All he'd ever been able to do with her was offer her shelter from whatever storm she was in—but he'd never been able to force her to accept it. For a year, he'd watched her stand on the outside of their group of friends like she wasn't quite sure she was welcome.

All he could do was keep holding his hand out to her, hoping she'd eventually take it. He'd thought that was actually happening last week.

Then why the hell did the fact that they were naked here together make him feel like they were growing further apart, not closer?

Her small fist wrapped around him, once again about to end this way too soon. He grabbed her hand and brought it up to his shoulder, then reached down under her thighs and lifted her so he could lay her out on the bed, ignoring the discomfort from his stitches.

If she couldn't or wouldn't tell him what was going on in her mind, then he would use this chance to show her how he felt. Show her she could trust him in the most basic way possible—with her body.

"Kendrick, I want you."

He kept his weight on his arms and lay on top of her, thrusting up against her, but not pushing inside. "Good, because you're going to get me. But not yet."

He kissed down her throat and her slim shoulders, taking ample time to familiarize himself better with those perfectly pert breasts. He slid one nipple into his mouth, alternating between sucks and little nips. His fingers tugged the other one.

Her gasps told him everything he needed to know. She

liked the little bite of pain more than gentle kisses. He wasn't surprised—nothing about Neo was typical.

But *everything* about her was damned near perfect for him.

He used both hands to tease her breasts—pinch, then stroke. Pinch until she gasped, stroke as she relaxed.

The feel of her squirming and the sound of her panting was doing nothing to slow this down like he'd planned. Watching her getting turned on was turning him on as much as her touch.

He let go of her breasts to kiss his way down her taut belly. He slid his hands down to her knees, then slowly trailed them back up her inner thighs.

"Kendrick . . ." Her voice was uneven. He'd never heard it like that—unsure, eager, breathy—and damned if it wasn't the sexiest thing he'd ever heard in his life.

"Woman, you've been driving me crazy since the first day I met you. Now it's time for me to return the favor for a moment."

His lips followed the same route his hands had taken, kissing from her knee up the sweet, soft skin of her thighs.

And then finally to the place he wasn't sure he'd ever want to leave.

He didn't show any mercy as he licked and tasted and devoured her. Whatever walls she might try to build to keep him out could not possibly stand under this onslaught, at least for these moments.

The sound of her sobbing his name, begging almost without coherence pushed him further. He drove her up and over the edge with his tongue, then added his fingers to wring another orgasm out of her, leaving her lying there a limp, shuddering mass.

Only then did he rise up on his knees, holding her legs open wide for him, and slide inside her, a groan falling from his throat.

She was tight and swollen from his attentions, and it felt so good, so damned right. He stared into her hazel eyes, loving how she was still a little dazed as he pushed the rest of the way inside her.

He kept his movements slow and easy, loving the way she felt around him. But when she shifted, hooking her legs around his waist, her hands gripping his shoulders, those short little nails digging into his skin, his control slipped. He thrust harder.

"It's time for fast and hard and deep, Blaze." She lifted her head and nipped his earlobe.

He shuddered. She wasn't the only one who liked a little bit of pain.

He slid his hand behind one of her knees and pushed her leg up higher, opening her more to him, and then let himself go—pounding into her, over and over. Her sighs and grunts and curses in his ears urged him on.

He chanted her name as waves of pleasure crashed over him way too soon, and *he* became the shuddering mass.

He was barely able to remove the condom and drop it in the trash before wrapping an arm around her waist and tucking her up against him. He couldn't stop his dazed sigh as sleep began to pull him under.

But even with her right next to him, with them having had been as close as two people could possibly be, he couldn't shake the feeling that she was still sliding away.

NEO KNEW she had to get up. Kendrick was behind her on his side wrapped around her like a damned octopus—one arm around her waist, the other under her neck and cupping her breast. He had one of his long legs between hers, his foot hooked over her ankle.

Like he *knew*. Like even in sleep, he knew she was going to try to get away.

She didn't want to move. Lying here like this should drive her crazy—it was the absolute epitome of violating personal space. But she loved it. Would've stayed there and slept for hours.

But she couldn't. She'd already stolen more time than she should. It had taken Kendrick longer than she'd thought it would to fall asleep. She'd planned to dash as soon as he did. But then she'd fallen asleep too.

And now he was snoring gently in her ear. He deserved the rest. She was exhausted and he'd been working for two days straight before she'd arrived.

She eased herself out of his grasp, everything about her feeling colder and emptier with each inch she distanced herself. She found her clothes and silently slipped them on, grabbing one of the shirts the guys had stocked the safehouse with.

She didn't look at Kendrick while she dressed. She couldn't. The jagged edges of her breaking heart were already slicing her to shreds. Looking at his sleeping form after what they'd just shared would be more than she could recover from.

She turned and walked toward the bedroom door.

"So that's it, huh? You're going to leave without saying goodbye at all?"

She froze at his words, but didn't turn around.

"We get this one time together and that's it?" he continued.

Now she turned to look at him but was careful not to meet his eyes. "How do you know I'm not running out to get us coffee? Breakfast?"

He sat up, bedsheet around his waist. "Because the only

thing more evident than the fact that what we just shared was freaking incredible was you using it to scream goodbye."

He knew her too damned well.

"It's better this way, Kendrick." She rubbed her forehead with her finger and thumb. She needed to get out of here before he started pressing her for answers that would destroy them both.

"You're honestly going to try to convince me it's better for you to sneak out? Was I ever going to see you again?" He stood up, gloriously unconcerned about his nakedness.

"There are things you don't know."

He shook his head. "There are *always* things someone doesn't know, Neo. But that doesn't mean you run. Whatever it is, we'll figure it out together."

He took a step toward her, arm outstretched, and she flinched. If he touched her now, she would crumble. She'd never be whole again.

Not that she would be anyway.

"So that's it?" He stopped. His hand dropped.

"It has to be this way."

"You know, I've never asked you for your secrets. I've never forced myself into the parts of your life you kept from everyone. I didn't want to scare you. I wanted it all to come naturally." He shook his head. "But maybe I should have pushed. If all we end up with is you running away anyway, maybe I should have."

She made the mistake of looking into those unique brown eyes. Found herself drowning in them, as always. She had to get out. If she didn't leave *right now*, she'd be watching those eyes turn cold.

"I'm sorry. More than you'll ever know. But I can't stay here anymore. Goodbye, Blaze."

She turned and ran.

He didn't try to stop her.

Chapter 17

Ray was well aware that the modified cabin in which she and Dorian lived was probably the only one of its type in the world. From the outside, it was nothing more than a hunter's weekend cabin. Nicer than the survival cabins like the one the kids currently resided in, which were really only meant for short-term stays in emergency situations, but not anything particularly fancy.

The weapons room and control center that could give her and Dorian up-to-date information about movement in any particular quadrant near them was one thing that made their cabin unique. The fact that it had two different underground exits through tunnels they'd built themselves was another unique factor. A hidden panic room with enough nourishment and weapons for them to survive for nearly a year was a third.

But the real reason, the greatest reason, this cabin of theirs was so unique was because of the luxurious shower Ray was currently standing in.

Indoor plumbing in these wilderness cabins was a rarity.

Luxury showers with rain-shower heads? Completely unheard of.

But Dorian had built this one for her because he knew how much she'd always loved showers. And a shower had been the turning point in their relationship when they'd discovered each other again a year and a half ago.

So he had engineered a way to divert water from the river to a collection tank near their house and use solar panels to keep it piping hot.

The only time they ever came close to running out of hot water was when Dorian joined her in the oversized shower covered in natural stone. By then, they probably needed a little cooling off anyway.

When she got out of the shower this time, Dorian was waiting, holding a towel open for her.

"I always love to see your face as you step out of that thing. There's never been anything so worth the effort in my entire life."

He kept the towel around her as she reached up on her tiptoes and kissed him. "You should've joined me."

"I knew you needed some time to think."

They both had. Trying to figure out what to do about Theo and Savannah was weighing on both of them. They hadn't done any deep searches for the kids' grandfather. Doing so might draw unwanted attention to both the kids and them. And since Ray—a.k.a. Grace Brandt, known terrorist—was officially dead, attention was something they tried to avoid at all costs.

But what if whoever had killed Grandfather came back for the kids?

Plus, even if there weren't bad guys potentially after them, Theo and Savannah couldn't stay in that cabin. They needed a home. Guardians. Regular food.

The American foster care system wasn't perfect, but it

was better than dying in the middle of the Wyoming wilderness. The kids would be placed in a family. She and Dorian would watch from a distance, from the shadows, to make sure they stayed safe and had good lives.

She and Dorian were too damaged to ever be parents themselves, but that didn't mean they were going to let anything happen to these kids. Theo and Savannah would grow up having a normal, happy life.

Ray and her crossbow would make sure of it. From a distance.

And if the thought of never being part of Savannah's and Theo's lives hurt Ray's heart a little, she ignored it. There was no room for sentimentality when it came to survival.

But they had a couple of months before the weather made it truly impossible for the kids to stay at the cabin. She and Dorian would make sure they had the food they needed and develop some sort of cover story for them. The last thing they wanted was for the kids to be deported back to Ukraine.

"I've got to practice baking."

Dorian smiled at her, then turned her around inside the towel so he could dry her off. She let him take care of her like this because it soothed something in both of them.

He rubbed the towel over her hair. "Your banana bread was . . . edible."

She elbowed his rock-hard abs. "It was more than edible. Barely." She laughed. It had been pretty bad. The kids had eaten it, but that wasn't saying much.

"Why don't you try something with chocolate? Brownies. Who cares about it being healthy? Give them a treat."

He hung up the towel as she stepped away and got dressed. "Yeah, brownies. What kid doesn't like brownies?"

"Exactly."

"We can make sure they have some healthy food to eat sometimes, but also give them some treats."

Maybe it would be enough to know she'd given them some smiles with her goodies once they were gone. Enough to ease this ache that was already starting in her chest.

She and Dorian looked through the pantry, trying to decide what they could make to take to the kids tomorrow and what would have to wait until after they'd had a chance to go back into town for supplies.

"The kids need some basics too, D. I don't want them going hungry while we figure out a long-term plan. We can get them some canned goods. And a camping stove so they can heat food more easily. Better utensils. I need to start a list."

He kissed the top of her head. "Good idea."

He was searching for a brownie recipe online, and she was writing ingredients on the list for their next trip into town when their perimeter alarm breach blared. They both dropped everything and ran over to the control screen.

There was a spot blinking, indicating where someone had tripped their alarm.

"That's the river," Dorian said. "But it's not where Theo usually puts his traps. He's never tripped the alarm before."

"Animal?"

They both watched the slight movement of the blinking light. "No. Whoever is there seems to be pacing back and forth."

She and Dorian looked at each other. Why would someone be pacing at the river?

They'd just seen the kids yesterday and had decided to wait until tomorrow to go again. After everything Theo and Savannah had shared about their past, Ray and Dorian hadn't wanted to push and cause them to panic and bolt. Trust took time.

But someone was pacing down at the river, which was the closest point between their two cabins. Whether it was one of the kids or someone else, it wasn't good news.

"Maybe we shouldn't have left them alone." Ray's hands balled into fists. "I know they're pretty self-sufficient, but ultimately they're still just kids."

"We'll get them a burner phone tomorrow when we go into town. Teach them how to use it. But right now let's figure out what the situation is and handle it."

He squeezed her shoulder. And she reached up and squeezed his wrist. Dorian was calm, focused. Today wasn't one of his bad PTSD days. Those had been coming less and less often.

The two of them balanced each other out. They always had.

"Let's go."

Thirty seconds later, they were armed and out the door, leaving Storm behind since they didn't know what they'd be facing. Neither of them spoke as they sprinted the three miles to the river. Normally they took much longer routes since they didn't want to leave any sort of worn path between the two cabins for someone to stumble across. Today, they took the shortest route possible.

A quarter mile from the river, Dorian veered off. Ray didn't have to ask what he was doing; they were too in tune with each other when it came to a mission like this. Dorian would be coming around from the outside, looking for any hidden dangers. He was the only person on earth she trusted enough to leave herself unguarded and bolt into a potentially deadly situation. She turned on the noise-blocking elements of her earbuds.

When Ray got close enough to see who was pacing at the river, she pushed herself for one last burst of speed, turning off the noise cancelation.

"Savannah! Savannah, what's wrong?" The little girl was sobbing. Ray ran up beside her and knelt down.

Savannah threw herself against Ray. "Theo cut himself. Bad. I can't get him to wake up."

Ray clicked her earpiece so she could talk to Dorian. "Did you hear that?"

"Already on my way."

Ray scooped up the little girl in her arms. "Why did you come here, sweetie?" To the river?"

"You and Dorian always come from the river. Your feet are wet when you arrive. And you reset our traps for us. I thought maybe you lived near here."

"Clever, clever girl." She kissed the top of Savannah's head. "Now let's get to your brother and help him. Dorian's already on his way."

Ray swung her around so the girl was on her back. Running with Savannah wasn't unlike running with a heavy backpack. Ray could take it. She'd do whatever was necessary to get to Theo and help him.

Having Savannah on her back reminded her of carrying little Jess to safety after a storm and mudslide a few months ago. Everything had turned out all right then, and damn it, it would turn out all right now. It had to.

Like Jess had been, Savannah was quiet too. The child heaved small sobs in Ray's ear but Savannah held on tight, making it easier for Ray to run. And Ray took advantage of it, moving with a surefooted speed that made her glad she and Dorian kept their bodies in fighting condition even when there didn't seem to be battles to fight.

By the time they got to the kids' cabin, Dorian was already there. He was kneeling by a still unconscious Theo.

Ray slid Savannah off her back and ran a hand down her hair. "You sit over here by the door sweetie, okay? That will give Dorian and me plenty of room to take care of Theo."

And because until she saw the wound for herself, she didn't want Savannah to be exposed to something even more traumatic. Savannah nodded and sat in the doorway, wrapping her arms around her little knees.

Ray went over and crouched beside Dorian. "Status?"

"He got himself good with that fucking knife. I'm assuming he was trying to skin an animal, miscalculated the force and cut all the way along his arm."

A small rag beside Theo was covered in blood. Dorian had already pulled out the first-aid supplies from the backpack he'd brought and was wrapping the ugly-looking gash with gauze.

"It must have happened a couple hours ago and neither of them knew what to do. He's probably out because of the combination of pain and blood loss, although I'm sure their current living situation didn't help things either." Dorian's voice was tight.

"Hospital?"

She kept her words brief, because all she really wanted to do was scream at both Dorian and herself for leaving the kids here alone, no matter how capable they seemed. Why had they done that?

"Probably. Let's get him back to our cabin and evaluate from there."

She walked back over to Savannah. "Honey, we think Theo needs to see a doctor. We're going to take him with us."

Savannah's little lip began to wobble. "I don't want to stay here by myself."

Ray snatched her against her chest. "No, of course not. We're not leaving you behind. You're coming with us. Let's pack what we can in a backpack so we can take it to my house."

Dorian had already stood and had Theo in his arms. "I'll get going."

"We'll be right behind you."

He caught her eyes and gave her a slow nod, a wealth of words in the simple movement:

It's going to be okay.

I love you.

We'll figure this out.

Her echoing nod said the same.

She helped Savannah gather what the girl felt was important—her clothes, Theo's clothes, their reading books, and even the knife Theo had cut himself with.

Savannah was preparing herself for them having to start over again alone.

Damned if Ray was going to allow that to happen.

"It won't all fit," Savannah said, after cramming her backpack full, obviously upset but trying to keep it together. "I'll take my books out."

"No." Ray grabbed her hands gently. "We'll carry the books together, okay? You don't need to leave them behind."

Savannah nodded, face lighting up with a wobbly smile. She began to sing some Ukrainian ditty Ray had heard them singing before. "*Che sim sim odyn, ju yee sist ju. Try em odyn. Sist che che sim.*"

"What song is that? I like it."

Savannah shrugged one little shoulder. "Grandfather taught it to us. It's a baby song. Is it okay if I like it? It reminds me of Grandfather."

Ray stroked a finger down her cheek. "Of course, sweetheart. Maybe you and Theo can teach it to me and Dorian." They got all the belongings and walked out the door. Ray pulled it closed behind her. "Sometimes silly songs are the perfect thing."

"Do you know any silly songs?"

Ray had to dig pretty damn deep to remember any nursery rhymes. Most of them, she was sure, were incorrect, but Savannah didn't seem to notice or mind as they walked. She liked "Row, Row, Row Your Boat" and "Twinkle, Twinkle Little Star" the most.

Ray alternated between carrying Savannah and letting her walk the miles back to the cabin. Dorian had taken the most direct route, not bothering to hide his trace in any way.

But there was no word from him in her headset. Did that mean good or bad news?

If they had to take Theo to the hospital, it was automatically going to put them in the system. The state would be involved and take custody. There wouldn't be much Ray and Dorian could do to interfere without being on the grid themselves.

She and Dorian had thought they had more time to figure out what would happen to the kids.

They'd been wrong.

DORIAN WAS DOING his damnedest to keep from jostling Theo too much. The kid being unconscious was probably a godsend. A cut like that had to hurt like hell.

The boy didn't weigh enough to be much of an issue as Dorian ran. He knew he was leaving a trail behind him that a three-year-old could follow, but he could go back and fix it later.

He was in the last half mile when he knew Theo was waking up. His little body was tense, stiffening against the pain.

"Hang in there, buddy," Dorian said near his head.

"Mr. Dorian?"

"It's me. You cut yourself, remember?"

"Where's Oksana? I mean—Savannah?"

Theo was in a shit ton of pain, but his first thought was still about protecting his sister.

You're a good man, kid.

"She's with Ray, right behind us. She's fine. We need to take you to the hospital."

Theo began to struggle for the first time in Dorian's arms. "No. No, please. No hospital."

Dorian slowed a little so he could talk more easily with the kid. "Theo, the cut on your arm is pretty bad. It needs to be seen by a doctor. You don't have to be afraid. They will give you medicine to make sure it doesn't hurt when they fix it."

Theo still struggled. "No, I can't go to the hospital. I can't."

This was more than the kid being afraid, or at least more than him being afraid of getting stitched up.

There was something Theo hadn't told them.

"Theo, I want to help you. But I need you to tell me everything you can. I'm not going to promise that we don't go to the hospital, because making sure you're okay is the most important thing. But if there's something I need to know, tell me so we can work this out together. Man to man."

Theo's face fell. "I'm not a man. I let Grandfather die."

Dorian doubted very much that Theo had done anything to *let* his grandfather die, but that wasn't the angle to take right now. "Believe me, kid. I've let people I love die too. It's an awful feeling, but you have to keep going. Like you've kept going for you and Savannah."

They were at the cabin. Dorian stopped at a nearby tree that served as a hidden security panel. He pressed his thumb against the scanner, then entered the code. It would shut down all the outer security measures. Ray would put them back up once she and Savannah were through.

He carried Theo inside and laid him down as gently as possible on the couch.

Theo still looked distraught. "Grandfather told me things that Savannah doesn't know. Told me I should never talk about it."

Tough position for an eleven-year-old to be in. "You were both protecting someone younger and more vulnerable. I respect that. But sometimes, we all have to choose to trust. I'd rather be able to show you this over time rather than say the words, but you can trust me. You can trust Ray also."

Theo nodded and sat up. Dorian didn't try to stop him even though it obviously hurt. "Grandfather said bad people would be looking for us. The same ones that hurt him. Said that they would try to get information from us."

"What type of information?"

"I'm not sure. Grandfather was trying to stop the bigger bad people." Theo shook his head, obviously frustrated that he didn't know more or have particulars. "When we first arrived in America and we were hiding, Grandfather left us at a hotel. He took his computer, and he went away. When he came back the next morning, he was very hurt. He'd been shot. I should've gone with him. But I wanted to stay and watch the American TV." Theo started to cry.

Dorian brushed his hand over the kid's head. "You couldn't have known. And even if you'd been there, it might not have made any difference at all. You could've been shot too."

The kid's eyes were still haunted. "Once Grandfather knew he was going to die, he made me promise to stay in the cabin as long as possible. Told me not to try to go to town or talk to any adults. To say we had just moved here, and that he would be coming back. No hospitals. No police. No one that will put you in the . . . sotsosvita. I don't know the English."

Dorian wasn't familiar with the word, but he got the gist. "He wanted to make sure you weren't in the system."

"Grandfather said the bad men would look for him, and that they would hurt us even if we told them he was dead." Theo grabbed Dorian's hand with his good one. "Please, no hospital."

"Okay. No hospital."

Relieved, Theo sank down into the couch. He'd been ready to run, Dorian realized. This was important enough to Theo that he would've made a break for it even with the shape he was in. Even knowing he probably wouldn't make it.

"But we're going to bring a doctor here, okay?"

Theo tensed again. "No. Grandfather said—"

Dorian put a hand on his shoulder. "I'm not going to let anyone take you. Not going to let anyone hurt you or Savannah. I promise. This is someone you can trust."

"Do you trust the doctor?"

"Yes, I trust her with my life. You can too."

Chapter 18

Kendrick didn't come after her. Neo shouldn't have expected him to. She'd told him to let her go. Then she'd walked out the door, leaving him standing there naked.

Had she really expected him to chase her? Run out into the driveway after her with no clothes on, asking her to come back? Telling her they could work it out?

Maybe some part of her had. That made her an *unreasonable* selfish bitch, rather than just a selfish bitch.

She took the car they'd driven to the Hemingway building last night since it was her only option. She'd have to find some way to get it back to them. Leave a message about where it was parked so Kendrick or one of the LT guys could come pick it up.

She drove back toward Oak Creek, eyes dry but burning, her body sore in the most delicious ways from Kendrick's lovemaking.

She shut those thoughts down hard. If she didn't, she wasn't going to be able to function. With each mile, she rebuilt the emotional wall that kept everything out.

She had survived alone before. She would survive alone again.

She was nearly all the way back to her house when she realized going there would be stupid. What if Varela was waiting? When she told him she wasn't going to help him anymore—that it didn't matter if he told all her friends about her surveillance cameras—he wasn't going to take that very well.

She wouldn't be any good to him. Not being any good meant no reason to keep her around.

She did a U-turn in the middle of the road, thankful no one else was around, and headed away from the town she'd called home. Anything at her house would have to be written off as a loss.

Or possibly, she could find a way to get back here for a few days once all this had blown over and Varela was sure she wasn't coming back. She could park far away and hike in through the wilderness. Varela wouldn't be expecting that.

Thinking about this, formulating a plan, was helping her pull herself together.

Focus on survival. There would be plenty of time to experience the agony from the gaping hole in her heart later. It wasn't going anywhere soon.

What did she need to survive this day? Most of it she could access online. IDs. Bank accounts—

Something rammed the back of the car and made her swerve off the road. The back wheels caught in the side ditch, almost making her lose control. What the hell?

She caught a glimpse of an SUV in the rear-view mirror before it rammed her again. She fought to stay on the road as it pulled up beside her. Varela smiled at her from the passenger seat.

Oh God.

The SUV rammed her from the side and knocked her

car all the way off the road this time. They weren't going to stop until they killed her.

There was no way she could make it back to town and no way to outrun them in this little car. She only had one option.

She slammed on the brakes with both feet and pulled the vehicle farther into the ditch. Then she jerked open the door and ran for the woods. It was her only chance.

The woods were her friend. She didn't know as much about hiding in them as the Linear Tactical guys, but maybe she'd be able to do enough to hide from Varela and his goons. If she could just reach the trees, she could disappear.

The squeal of brakes behind her told her she didn't have much time. She let out a curse as the sound of the vehicle got louder rather than fading away. They weren't chasing after her on foot, they were taking their SUV off road.

She wasn't going to make it. Even pushing for as much speed as she could, there was no way she could make it deep enough into the tree line to hide herself.

She pushed anyway.

She barely heard the sound of a door slamming over her sobbing breath. Someone yelled, but she didn't slow down.

She knew it was inevitable, but the flying tackle still took her by surprise as it forced her to the ground, knocking all the air from her lungs.

"Fucking bitch. You're lucky Varela wants you alive."

Hugo. *Shit.*

She tried to turn and hit out with her elbows, but Hugo was using his significant weight to crush her. She couldn't even get in a breath. The world was graying out around her when he finally shifted enough to allow air into her lungs. Before she could even appreciate not dying, he snatched her up by the hair, forcing her to stand as he did.

"I'm not particularly athletic, Neo." Varela walked

toward them, flicking a leaf off his jacket sleeve. "I'm glad Hugo caught you when he did so that I didn't have to ruin my five-hundred-dollar shoes. That would not have boded well for you."

"Hugo. Right. I'd forgotten his name." Neo forced the terror out of her voice. "I generally just think of them as Goon One and Goon Two."

Varela chuckled and nodded. "Clever. I do so like clever people. I spend a lot of time around not so clever"—he held out a hand toward Hugo and Porter—"so intelligence is appreciated."

He gave a short nod at Hugo and before she was aware of what might happen, a fist crashed into her midsection.

All the oxygen was sucked off of the planet. She doubled over, trying to force air back into her starving system.

"Of course, Hugo and Porter are very good at following orders. Unlike you. I haven't heard from you in quite a while, Neoma. I thought we had a deal."

Neo forced herself to stand up straight. "Oh, that's right, I forgot to send you the information I have for you." She was about to make things worse but couldn't stop herself. She acted like she was reaching into her pocket for something, then pulled her hand out, flipping Varela the bird. "Here it is. Found it."

The fist that crashed into the side of her face sent her sprawling to the ground. She could taste blood as her teeth cut the inside of her cheek. A booted foot kicked her in the thigh. She couldn't stop her cry as agony shot up her leg.

"Enough, Hugo. We can't take a chance on anybody driving by and seeing her car on the side of the road. You two take her to her house in her car. I'll follow in ours."

Hugo drove while Porter kept an iron-clad grip on her arm. Maybe he wasn't so stupid, because if he hadn't been holding her, the first chance she got she would've dived out of the vehicle. She prayed they would pass someone—*anyone*—on the way to her house. All she had to do was get one person's attention and everyone in this damn town would be talking about how Neo was going behind Kendrick's back with not one, but *two* men.

But what did it matter? If a nosy neighbor called Kendrick, he would merely say he and Neo meant nothing to each other anymore.

She'd made that clear to Kendrick, hadn't she? That she wanted nothing to do with him.

The cavalry wasn't coming. She needed to focus on saving herself. Varela hadn't killed her yet, but as soon as she told them she wasn't going to help them anymore, that would probably change.

When the car stopped, Porter dragged her inside by the hair. After Varela entered, Hugo locked the front door behind him and stood in front of it with his arms crossed.

She turned to face Varela. "I'm not going to help you with this anymore. I know about Mosaic. I know what they do—the human trafficking. The caging people. I don't care if you show my friends the surveillance stuff; I'm still not going to help you."

She did care. But it wasn't going to matter. She'd be gone, so she wouldn't have to see all their disappointed faces when they found out what she'd done. Who she really was.

She crossed her arms over her chest. "So basically you can kiss my ass."

She expected this blow. Too bad it was on the back of her head. What she wanted was so many bruises that if she was forced to work with anyone from Linear Tactical, they would immediately know she was being coerced.

But Varela had thought of that also. "No more marks on the face, Porter. And no head trauma. We need Neo to slip back in without questions being asked."

Porter grabbed her by the hair and threw her to the ground. His first kick crashed into her hips. She tried to scurry away, but a second kick caught her in the same place.

The pain exploded, and she fell back to the ground as a third kick nailed her between the shoulder blades.

She stopped counting, stopped trying to remain stoic as the pain continued. Not crying out wasn't an option. She curled up as small as she could, just trying to survive. Blow after blow.

Survive.

It took her a long moment to realize when Porter finally stopped. She was barely hanging on to consciousness. She stayed curled in her ball, struggling to breathe. The entire lower half of her body felt like it was on fire.

Varela crouched down beside her. "Porter has a unique gift, doesn't he?" She heard his words like he was talking to her through multiple panes of glass. "No broken bones. No shots to the kidney that would require an emergency trip to the hospital. No obvious bruises that you're going to have to explain away. Just a lot of pain."

She let out a groan as Varela rolled her until she was facing him.

"You're going to help us, Neo. Do you want to know why?"

She could barely think around the fog of suffering stealing her breath, much less answer.

"Porter likes pain. I don't have as much a stomach for it, maybe because I've never had to depend on my strength to get what I want. I use my real muscles." He tapped his temple.

She closed her eyes.

"Neo." Varela's voice was so even. So reasonable. "We both know how this is going to play out, don't we? You're not equipped to withstand this. A few more kicks and you're going to agree to do whatever I ask, because that's the smart thing to do."

She grunted, refusing to answer. But he wasn't wrong. She'd promise anything if it kept Porter away from her.

"You have no options here, right now," Varela continued. "But you're brilliant. So in a second you'll agree—or pretend to agree—in order to open up *future* potential options. That's what a survivor does."

He was right again.

"But I'm smart too. And I know as soon as we're gone, you'll run. Hide. Disappear. Isn't that what you're an expert at? Getting what you want, then disappearing without a trace? You've made a living out of it. At least that's what my sources tell me."

"If you know all this, why don't you just kill me?" She got the words out through gritted teeth. She'd only taken one blow to the face but talking still hurt.

God, everything hurt. She hadn't known this sort of pain was possible.

He smiled. "The key to getting people to do the work you want is to find out what their pressure points are. I thought yours was your little band of friends here, and how you'd potentially betrayed them. But evidently that wasn't quite enough."

He nodded at Porter and Neo shrank back as he walked toward her, but all he did was help her sit up. The world spun, everything turning gray, and she was pretty sure she was going to vomit everywhere. But retching would just cause more pain, so she forced herself to breathe as the world finally settled around her.

"You're going to help us." Varela tapped something on his phone and spun it so Neo could see. "Because I know where you were last weekend."

Whatever fight she might have had, whatever plans she'd

been considering, disappeared at the sight of the picture Varela showed her. Her shoulders slumped, head hanging down, as bile burned the back of her throat—a very different kind of pain this time.

Varela had won. Checkmate when she hadn't even known they were past the first few moves.

"There you go. I knew you could be reasonable." His voice was friendly, paternal. Made her want to vomit again.

Varela waved the phone back and forth. "These people are your pressure point. If you don't help us, then I'm going to turn Porter loose on *them*. He'll hurt them, Neo. Kill them if I tell him to. Painfully. They'll be unfortunate casualties in a war they know nothing about."

Neo didn't know how he had found them. She'd made sure her online persona, her hacking, her electronic signature, was never linked to them.

But she'd gotten sloppy last weekend when she'd gone to visit. It wouldn't have been terribly difficult for someone with computer savvy and access to camera networks to trace Neo back to where she'd been.

From there, it was just a matter of identifying who they were, how they were linked to her. Not easy, but not impossible either.

Varela had obviously done that.

"Fine," she whispered. "I'll do what you want."

Porter looked disappointed as he helped her get to her feet. She didn't want to touch him, but there was no way she could get up on her own. Her entire body felt swollen and slow as she hobbled to her kitchen, gripping the counter for support so she could make it to one of the chairs at her small table. Standing for very long wasn't going to be an option.

She told Varela everything he wanted to know—couldn't think clearly enough through the pain to hold back strategic info. Most of his questions were about Dr. Sevier. She told him about the flight from Europe to Salt Lake City and how he'd disappeared after that. She told him about Hemingway Travel Agency and how she'd stopped Kendrick from accessing the drive.

Varela looked pleased. Evidently tracking down Dr. Sevier was of the utmost priority to him. Neo hated to provide Varela with information that might lead to Sevier's capture, but she didn't have any choice in the matter.

She couldn't protect Dr. Sevier. Not when it might come at the cost of the lives of the people in the picture Varela had shown her.

The people in that photo—one in particular—were innocent, not a part of any of the bad or dangerous things Neo had let herself get involved with over the years. They weren't tied to any of her sins.

There was nothing she wouldn't do to protect them.

She gave Varela as much info as she could, whatever kept him looking pleased, but tried not to give everything. But she was still giving him way too much.

Finally, after hours of answering his questions, Varela was satisfied she'd provided him with all the information she could.

She'd saved a little, but only because she'd need something to report later. There was no way Kendrick was going to let her waltz back in and work with him again after this morning. She couldn't worry about that right now.

"Since you can't be trusted to contact us with information, you're going to keep this with you at all times." Varela handed her a burner phone. "Once you've located Dr. Sevier, you will notify me, then you'll bring me the drive. You can't be trusted to destroy it. Porter is leaving now for Denver. If I don't hear from you every twelve hours with updates, then somebody there gets hurt. "

Without another word, they left.

Neo sat staring at the table, unable to get up if she wanted to. There was nothing on the flat surface, but in her mind she could still see two images—that teenager from Ian's file that Mosaic had trapped, and the photo Varela had flashed in front of her.

Two innocents. If she helped one, she was damning the other. One lived. One died.

She couldn't see a way out of it. *She* was the weapon that was going to be used against innocents.

Unless . . . she destroyed the weapon altogether.

It had been a long time since she'd had any real thoughts of suicide. As a young teenager, when so much of her life had seemed to be spiraling out of her control, she'd considered it. Darkness and depression had threatened to swamp her psyche more than once.

She'd even gone as far as to hack into the system and write a prescription for sleeping pills for herself. Bottle in hand, she'd come close to taking her own life.

But in the end, she hadn't—mostly because she'd chickened out. She'd always been thankful that she'd held on to life.

But now . . .

The two images floated in front of her vision once more. Maybe she didn't have to hurt either. She could take herself completely out of the equation.

Permanently.

Varela would have no need to carry through on his threat against . . . innocent parties. And she could send a message to Kendrick, one he wouldn't get until she was gone, explaining that she'd held him back but he'd been closer to cracking the drive than he'd thought. She'd already left him one message. Had he figured that one out yet?

Every part of her body hurt as she slumped deeper into

the chair. She could have the pills in her hand before she needed to report to Varela.

Nobody else needed to get hurt because of her.

Maybe this was the best way.

The only way.

Chapter 19

Kendrick got back in bed and lay staring at the door for a long time after Neo left, his mind running over everything.

What the hell had happened? The best sex of his life by far, then she'd literally run out the door.

He'd always known she had secrets. Hell, she'd fairly dripped with them when they'd first met. Some of those secrets he knew. Even some of the ones she didn't think he did.

The others he'd made his peace with, accepting he would probably never know. Not unless she wanted to tell him. And he'd made sure she'd known that—that they were hers to tell or hers to keep.

He'd done his damnedest not to push—to give her a place, a person, where she could feel safe, even knowing she might never share everything about herself. He'd been okay with that. Having Neo with secrets was better than no Neo at all.

At any given time, Kendrick was surrounded by all these alpha warrior Linear dudes who were constantly ready to fight their way through any situation. Break through any wall. Charge through any chasm. Brute force whenever the situation called for it, and sometimes even when it didn't.

Kendrick respected that mindset, but that wasn't his way. He liked to use his brain first and foremost. And his people skills. He liked to smile, to charm, to get to know someone.

He'd thought that was working with Neo, at least getting her comfortable enough to stick around even if she was never going to spill her guts.

But evidently, he wasn't nearly as charming as he thought he was. Because he had no doubt that what had happened here this morning was a permanent goodbye.

Finally, he forced himself to get up. He was going to have to figure out a way to crack this drive without her help.

And that was what was bothering him the most, wasn't it? Not that she didn't want to be with him—hell, maybe he'd misread her response and the sex hadn't been that great for her. That was a blow to his pride, sure, but recoverable.

But the fact that she could walk away in the middle of them trying to stop Mosaic right after Ian had shown them exactly what they were really up against?

That was a level of aloofness he would not have thought her capable of.

He got dressed, put on a pot of coffee, and sat down at his backup computer. He wasn't sure where to start. He was further behind than he'd been before they'd broken into the travel agency since his primary computer with any data they'd had was gone. Not that it had held anything useful anyway. But still, he'd have to rebuild and start again.

It still seemed so impossible that between the two of them they'd made so little progress on the drive in three days. Maybe restarting from the beginning—*fucking again*—was best. Painful, but best.

He was only a few minutes into it when his fingers froze

on the keyboard. On the table at the far end of the room sat Neo's laptop. She'd left it here.

He stared at it for a long minute, trying to wrap his head around any possible reason she would have done that.

Forgetting it wasn't an option. There was no way she could've been upset enough that she would've forgotten her laptop if she was leaving for good.

She'd left it here.

He gave his mind free rein to spin through the possible ramifications. None of what he came up with was good.

"Please, Neo. Please, please, tell me this does not mean what I think it means."

He walked toward the laptop like it was a ticking bomb. That was an apt enough description.

But what it really was, was *evidence*.

He picked it up but didn't open it. He didn't have the equipment needed to crack it here, and someone of Neo's level of expertise would have a failsafe ready to wipe her drive clean if he tried.

Why leave it here at all?

He sat back down on the couch with his computer, retracing their electronic steps for the past three days—but this time through the lens of her *hindering* him rather than helping.

Through that lens, everything made sense.

The reason why it had seemed like someone was inside his brain, predicting everything he would do and stopping him? The new player he'd thought had entered the scene?

All Neo.

She'd betrayed him. Betrayed them all.

His foot shot out and kicked over the coffee table. He winced at the pull on his stitches but didn't care. He wanted to do much more than topple one small table. He wanted to tear down this entire place with his bare hands.

Why would she do this? This went so much further than having secrets.

He got up and moved the laptop to the kitchen table. Throwing a temper tantrum wouldn't solve anything. The opposite. He needed to use his brain. He needed to eliminate emotion completely and focus on undoing whatever damage Neo had done.

It all came down to this Dr. Sevier guy. That was the only thing she'd allowed them to move forward with unfettered. Was she working for him? Ian had said Dr. Sevier wasn't part of Mosaic, but did they know that for a fact?

All Kendrick knew for sure was that they needed Sevier to provide that fucking fifteen-digit code and DNA to open the drive outside of a Mosaic-operated building. Getting back into the travel agency would be nearly impossible now.

He scrubbed a hand over his head. Was Dr. Sevier working for Mosaic? God, was *Neo* working for Mosaic?

No. *Right?*

She'd been just as shocked and disgusted as he'd been when Ian had shown them those photos and told them what was going on. Neo could have some pretty questionable judgment when it came to hacking and making money.

But assisting in human trafficking? He couldn't believe that was the case.

He needed fucking answers. And he was damned well going to get them.

He grabbed a mug of coffee, gulped it down, nearly searing his throat, and got back to work on his computer. He was about to do something he'd told Neo he'd never do, and to this point, he had kept his word.

Because he'd wanted to let her know it was okay if she had secrets. Because he'd wanted her to know she could trust him.

It was time to find out where Neo lived.

It didn't take long to find the info, despite the traps she'd set that would catch anyone else.

But she hadn't been trying to keep him from finding out, had she? The true test had been whether he would honor her wishes.

He couldn't believe it when her address flashed up on his screen less than five minutes later. She lived just outside *Oak Creek*.

He sat back staring at the screen, shaking his head. He would've bet all his money she lived in Reddington City—that she would want to be somewhere with more anonymity. She'd certainly done a good job keeping her house a secret. Someone fooling him with such thoroughness was a rarity.

And she'd done it twice in one day. Maybe he really didn't know her at all.

He rubbed his chest. It was aching way more than last night's wound. Like there was a hole, a missing part of him. A feeling like he'd lost something precious before he'd even had a chance to really have it.

If Neo lived in Oak Creek, then she must have taken the car. A quick check on its GPS location confirmed that he had the right address. The car was parked there. Hopefully, she was still there too.

He grabbed his phone. He hated to bring in anyone else, but defeating Mosaic was more important than keeping the fact that he'd been a fool and Neo had played him perfectly.

He called Ian. "I figured out why I haven't been able to crack the drive yet. And I need you to bring me a car."

Chapter 20

Thirty minutes later, Kendrick was parked in front of Neo's house. The safe house car was parked in the driveway. Lights were on behind the blinds in the window. She was still here.

Ian had gotten Kendrick the vehicle he needed, but it had required Kendrick filling him in about Neo.

The fact that Ian had been willing to let Kendrick sort through this himself spoke volumes about the other man's control. Kendrick hadn't outright said Neo was a traitor, wasn't willing to say that until he had absolute proof, but they both knew the circumstances pointed in that direction. Ian hadn't insisted on taking control of the situation and finding Neo himself, and that was out of respect for Kendrick.

Respect or not, he had no doubt Ian had some sort of backup plan. He wouldn't be surprised if there were eyes on him and this house right now. Ian would do whatever it took to take down Mosaic.

Kendrick knocked on Neo's door and waited, staring at her cute little house with its well-maintained flower beds and shrubbery. She'd spent hours in this yard, and he'd never known about it.

It took her so long to answer he thought she wasn't going to. The door finally cracked open. He was ready to have it slammed in his face when she saw it was him, but to his surprise she opened it more fully.

"I found you." He walked inside.

She stood clutching the door. "I see that. I never actually doubted you'd be able to."

He was done with charming and friendly. This rage eating at him didn't allow for either. But his voice remained even. "Given how stupid I've been, I'm surprised. All logical assumptions when it comes to you and me lead straight to *Kendrick is an idiot*."

She didn't respond as he surveyed her house. Not what he was expecting, although honestly, what *had* he been expecting? Maybe a bachelorette's pad? Sparse, functional.

Instead it was cozy—throw pillows and knickknacks and paintings. Not enough to be cluttered, just enough to feel . . . homey. Fresh flowers overflowed a vase on the console table in the hall. Like the outside, she'd taken her time in this house. Put her mark on it.

He spun around to face her again. "I finally figured it out."

She'd shut the door but otherwise hadn't moved. Any other time he would've taken a moment to appreciate that she was standing in a green cotton robe that barely came down to her knees. It looked soft. As soft as her skin.

Evidently, he'd interrupted her taking a bath.

That fucking said it all, didn't it? That she could just relax and *take a bath* right now in the middle of this?

"You misled us about Mosaic for three damned days, doing everything you could to make sure I wouldn't crack that drive." He spit the words through ground teeth, starting to pace. "And your conscience was clear enough to just come home and loll around in the tub?"

She didn't say anything.

"Are you working for Dr. Sevier? Covering for him? Is he paying you? How much?" Not that it mattered. He scrubbed his hands over his head. "Jesus, Neo. Are you working directly for Mosaic? After everything Ian told us about what they do? The pictures we saw?"

Still nothing from her. He stopped pacing and stared at her, one eyebrow raised. He waited for her smartass answer because he knew she had one. A snippy comeback about how a girl's got to eat or some such shit.

He wanted her to fight with him. To get all up in his face and tell him that he should have been able to see around her when cracking that drive. That she'd been trying to point out his weaknesses.

God, more than anything he wanted her to have a good reason for having betrayed him. Betrayed *all* of them— including those souls living in hell on Earth, trapped by Mosaic.

But she just stood there quietly in the foyer.

"Nothing?" he asked. "You have *nothing* to say for yourself?"

"I told you there were things about me you didn't know." Her voice sounded stiff, off.

"Then fucking *tell me*." He threw his arms up in the air and took a couple of steps closer, wanting her to flip him off, or poke him in the chest and tell him to cut the holier-than-thou shit.

But she flinched and stepped back, drawing in on herself. Like he was going to *hurt* her. Like after everything they'd been through, he was going to lay a hand on her.

And damned if that didn't hurt most of all.

He lowered his arms and took a step back, shaking his

head. "I should've known not to trust you. Way back when I found you'd placed surveillance devices in our friends' homes."

She sucked in a little breath. "You knew about that?"

He rolled his eyes. "Are you kidding? I fed you false info on them starting from day one—you obviously weren't listening closely or you would've caught the loops."

"I—" She swallowed. "I—"

"Then a couple weeks later, you shut them down. None of them were actually transmitting, so I figured it was some sort of security blanket for you. Trying to make sure everyone was who they seemed while you made a place for yourself here. I guess I was wrong. I guess you've proven —*again*—that you're only good at looking out for yourself."

Still, she said nothing. Just stood there looking like *she* was the wounded one.

He had to get out of here. It had been a mistake to come here in the first place. He'd been looking for something she was never going to give him. "Goodbye, Neo."

"Goodbye." Her voice was no more than the tiniest of whispers.

She barely moved as he brushed by her, went back out to the car, and got inside. He couldn't waste any more time here, not if she was giving him the silent treatment—a first, that was for sure.

He needed to walk away and undo the damage she'd done. Ian would have to send in someone more neutral to talk to her and get the details of all the ways she'd sabotaged this mission.

He started the car, then turned it off again, slamming his fist down on the steering wheel multiple times.

Goddammit. Why hadn't she argued with him? Why hadn't she told him to go fuck himself, that she'd never claimed to be one of the good guys, and that if she'd blinded him, then that was his own fault, wasn't it?

She hadn't. But more . . .

Why had she looked afraid? He'd never once seen Neo look afraid in all the months he'd known her. Not like this.

Kendrick had been raised by two parents who were opposites in a lot of ways. His mother was a surgeon, her passion and empathy for her patients evident in everything she did. His father, the judge, tended to set emotion aside entirely and focus on the details that mattered—using a sense of logic and cool reasoning to cut through often emotional legal quagmires.

Kendrick tended naturally to be like his mother—more outgoing and passionate. But right now, he needed to draw from Dad: logic, focus, attention to detail. And those things told him there was more going on with Neo than what he understood.

He was missing something. Neo didn't sit meekly while someone yelled at her and then calmly say goodbye. She didn't flinch, even when she was doing something immoral.

And, damn it, she did not work for Mosaic. He knew that down in the very core of himself.

He'd seen her face when Ian talked about what Mosaic did and when she'd seen those pictures. No one was that good of an actress. She'd been as disgusted as he was.

Neo didn't work for Mosaic—there was something else at play. But maybe she was doing what she always did: trying to carry too much herself. Trying to solve any problem she had on her own. She'd never had anyone else to help her shoulder her burdens.

She might not accept his help now if she was in trouble, but damn it, he was at least going to offer. He got back out of the car. He needed to know exactly what was going on here.

He knocked on the door but didn't wait for her to answer before going inside. "Dammit, Neo, I know you're not working for Mosaic. So you tell me what the hell is going on—"

Opposite the front door, Neo stood in her kitchen. He stopped when she spun with a knife in her hand.

There were multiple things wrong with this scenario. She wasn't normally so jumpy that someone calling out to her from across a room would cause her to panic and spin with a knife.

But the bigger problem was the lack of grace with which she moved. So unlike her.

And then there was the way the color bled from her face, leaving her pale as death.

Oh fuck. "You're hurt," he whispered.

"I thought you were gone."

He took slow steps toward her. She still had that knife in her hand. That tight look on her face.

Something was very, very wrong.

"I came back because none of this is adding up." He kept his voice low, steady.

But it was starting to add up now. As he reached her, he took the knife from her hand—she made no effort to resist whatsoever—and set it on the counter. He studied her face, then reached up and touched her lips, which were the slightest bit swollen.

And not in a good way.

She tried to turn away from him but winced at the movement.

She was hurt *bad*. Somewhere in the lower half of her body. He stepped back and lifted the hem of her robe. He only had to shift it a couple of inches before the bruises beginning to mottle the outside of her thigh became visible.

"Neo." He eased the material farther aside, sucking in a

breath. Her hip and upper thigh, her shoulders . . . Swollen and red, with bruising that would be deep purple and black in a few hours.

Someone had kicked her repeatedly and had done so since she'd left him this morning.

He looked her in the eyes. "Do you need a hospital?"

She shook her head the slightest bit.

He wanted to pull her into his arms. Demand answers. But instead he cupped her cheek with both hands.

"You have secrets. Okay. But you're not in this alone anymore."

Chapter 21

Kendrick helped Neo collect her stuff. He didn't ask any questions, unsure if her house was a safe place to talk.

She was so stiff and in so much pain, he had to help her get dressed. Neither of them said anything, but the bruises flowering all over her back, hips, and legs made it clear how badly she'd been beaten.

It didn't take long for him to realize it had been strategic. Someone had wanted to cause her a lot of pain without making it obvious she'd been beaten.

If he'd thought the rage he'd felt when he'd entered her house was strong, it was nothing compared to what he was feeling now.

Rage at the people who had done this, at himself for almost missing it, and, to a much lesser degree, with Neo for not coming to him in the first place. For putting herself in a position where she'd had to endure so much pain.

He tamped it all down. Right now, the only important thing was taking care of her. He got her into the car and backed out of her driveway.

"There's no need to go back to the safe house. They're

not going to attack. They want us to find more info on Dr. Sevier." Her voice was hoarse, defeated. She stared out the window.

He turned to take her to his house rather than going back toward Reddington City.

"I have to report in every twelve hours." She held out a burner phone but never looked away from the window.

"Can you talk?"

"I don't have surveillance devices on me if that's what you mean."

"Who did this to you?" His hands tightened on the steering wheel. It was hard to focus on anything but finding who'd done this and making them pay—blow for blow.

"The guy who ordered it is Silas Varela. He works for Mosaic—has been tasked with finding Dr. Sevier."

"That explains why Dr. Sevier was the only area in which we made progress."

She shrugged one shoulder, still looking out the window. "Yeah. And now I'm supposed to take him the drive once we find Dr. Sevier."

"He's been hurting you the whole time? Blackmailing you?"

"Blackmail first—threatening to tell you and all of Linear about the surveillance I set up."

"We already knew about that."

She rubbed her eyes. "But I didn't know you knew. I thought you wouldn't want anything to do with me anymore if you knew. I thought I could . . . manage things."

Kendrick shook his head, keeping his eyes on the road. "You thought you could play both sides. Give Varela enough intel to keep him happy, work with me to make some progress, but ultimately stop me from accessing the drive."

"Yes," she whispered. "If it helps at all, I didn't know exactly what we were dealing with at first. I knew Mosaic was bad, but I didn't truly understand until this morning, when Ian and Landon told us."

"So you thought you would run. Take yourself out of the equation."

"Yes. But Varela and his men caught me when I came back into town. Decided a demonstration of violence would be more effective."

He gripped the steering wheel so tightly his knuckles turned white. "Well, I can fucking guarantee you that that's not going to happen again. I'm not going to allow it. Nobody at Linear or Zodiac is going to allow it. Varela isn't going to lay another finger on you. I promise you that."

He didn't expect her to gush her thanks. Neo was no damsel who needed rescuing. But he didn't expect her brief whisper. "No. You can't help me."

"Damn it, Neo. There's a fucking difference between being rescued and allowing your friends to stand shoulder to shoulder with you to fight the enemy. This isn't something you have to do alone."

He pulled up in front of his house and turned to stare at her. He wasn't getting out until she understood they would fight for her. *With* her. All of them.

"That's not the issue," she finally said. "There are other factors in play. Things I can't tell you."

More secrets.

He studied her face. Her eyes didn't meet his. *Other factors* meant Varela was threatening more than just her—threatening something or someone she loved.

It hurt him to think he had no idea who or what that could possibly be.

"Okay," he finally said. It was hard to say the word, but he had to work within the parameters he was given.

If she couldn't, or wouldn't, tell him what Varela was

holding over her, then Kendrick would have to work around it.

"*Okay?*" she asked. "That's it. After everything I've done?"

"Right at this second, we're going to worry about taking care of you. The rest can come later."

She tried to get out of the car herself but had stiffened while sitting on the ride over. He walked around and lifted her out of the car as gently as possible. Tears still leaked out of her eyes even though she didn't voice any complaints.

"Let me call and get you something for the pain." Damn it, he should've thought of that earlier. She looked so small and fragile in his arms. And the tears running down that strong face were ripping his heart out.

"No. Just give me a few ibuprofen. I'll be okay."

He carried her all the way into his bedroom and tucked her into his bed. There she finally struggled. "No, we have to work. I have to report in in ten hours. I have to, Kendrick. It's not an option."

He reached down and kissed her forehead. "I'm going to need you to do something that doesn't come very easily for you."

"What?"

"Trust me. You have to rest, give your body and mind a little time to recover. Trust that I will have you awake before the ten hours is up, and I will have something for you to report back to this asshole."

She stared at him, those big hazel eyes blinking. "Why are you helping me?"

He brushed a strand of hair back from her forehead. "Your secrets are part of you, Neoma. I've known that from the day we met. I hope to spend a great deal of time when this is all over convincing you to share those secrets with me so they can't ever be used against you again. But for right now, I need you to rest and then get back into fighting shape so we can figure this out, together."

She nodded. "All of it."

He kissed her forehead again. "That's right. All of it. We figure out how to fool the people trying to control you. We figure out how to crack this drive. And we figure out how to shut these motherfuckers at Mosaic down. That's going to take both of us—but I have no doubt that with both of us working toward the same goal, there will be no stopping us."

Chapter 22

Theo was going to be okay.

Dorian had never actually questioned that even when he'd been running with the unconscious kid in his arms. The boy was a fighter and had too much to live for—someone special who needed him around—to give up.

Dorian knew the feeling.

That feeling had gotten Dorian through more than one PTSD episode in the past couple of years, knowing that Ray needed him as healthy and whole as he could be. Sometimes you couldn't be strong for yourself. But you always found a way to be strong for the people you loved.

Anne Mackay had come to the house to stitch Theo up, brought by her husband, Zac. To say they'd both been shocked to find Dorian and Ray at the cabin with two children would be a complete understatement.

Zac was one of Dorian's oldest and best friends. He'd been the leader of the five friends who'd followed Dorian into the wilderness a few years ago when things had gotten their worst with his PTSD. They'd found him, stayed with him, led him as gently as possible back into the fold.

He and Zac had seen all sorts of highs and lows together. Multiple times they'd been pretty damn sure they weren't getting out alive. But they had.

Zac sat outside with Dorian now. Ray was with Savannah, keeping the little girl occupied picking flowers while Anne worked on Theo's arm inside. Neither Anne nor Theo had wanted an audience while she stitched him up.

"You've got two kids running around your house, Ghost." Zac shook his head. "I'm not sure I ever thought I'd be saying those words to you."

"Trust me when I say I never thought I'd be hearing them from you."

Kids had never been on Dorian's radar. There had never been anyone he wanted to have kids with besides Ray. For a long time, it had looked like she was dead. Then, when he'd discovered she wasn't and they'd come back into each other's lives, she'd eventually informed him that kids weren't an option for her. When she'd found out Project Crypt had been using her for missions without her permission—some of a sexual nature—she'd had her tubes tied to make sure pregnancy would never be an issue.

Dorian hadn't even mourned the fact that they would never have kids. He'd had Ray, and that was enough. More than he'd ever thought he would have.

But he knew Ray had mourned it.

Dorian let out a sigh. "I know Anne has questions about Theo and Savannah. We're trying to figure out what to do with them."

He explained it all to Zac, all the details he knew about the kids and how they'd gotten here.

Zac didn't judge, merely promised to look into it. Nobody wanted two innocent kids hunted down and hurt. But obviously, they couldn't stay in that cabin alone.

"Okay, all stitched up." Anne walked out to where he

and Zac were standing. "Tough kid. I gave him a tetanus booster but would like to see both of them for full a checkup sometime soon. I can do it myself."

Dorian hugged her. "I'll let Zac fill you in on the details. We're trying to figure out what to do with them—how to keep them safe."

Anne gave them her soft, gentle smile. "I'll go pack up my stuff then. I need to get back to the hospital."

Zac nodded and turned to Dorian as she walked back into the house. "This danger with the kids . . . does it have anything to do with the tangos that showed up here last week? Mosaic?"

"No. We haven't had any sign of bad guys anywhere around here. Ray and I have these woods monitored all over the place, and nothing has been tripped. How's Kendrick been doing with the drive?"

"He ran into a couple of unexpected snags, but he's still working on it."

Anne gave him a few medical instructions before they left, nothing too complicated. Ray stood next to Dorian as they waved goodbye. Savannah was showing Theo the flowers she'd picked. Theo seemed good as new, although Anne had left some painkillers if he needed them.

Ray leaned in closer as they looked at the kids in the soft light of sundown. "I'm setting up the extra room for them to sleep in. I can't send those kids back to that cabin alone. Not tonight."

He wrapped an arm around her shoulder. "I know. Me neither. Tonight they stay here with us."

TWO DAYS LATER, the kids were still at Ray and Dorian's house. He was sitting on a tree stump near their front door,

Ray in his lap. For the first time, he wished they had more of a traditional porch or something. Rocking chairs, so they could watch the kids play.

They'd never even considered it because it would immediately tag their cabin as being more developed and inhabited than either of them had wanted it to appear at first glance.

Plus, traditional domestic life had never been what they'd envisioned for themselves.

"That's what they're supposed to be doing," Ray said softly. "Not thinking about anything but playing."

The kids were laughing and singing their silly song as they played—literally chasing butterflies flying around them.

He and Ray could almost sing their little nursery rhyme now too. Maybe they should learn some more Ukrainian songs.

Theo and Savannah had spent the past two days being normal kids. They hadn't had to catch their own food. They'd read their books. They'd spent time in the kitchen together baking. Thankfully, it had turned out much better than the original banana bread.

Theo's arm was healing well. Probably because the kid could get a good night's sleep and not have to worry about being his sister's sole line of protection.

Dorian and Ray, on the other hand, had been awake almost the entire night last night. Both of them knew they needed to find a permanent home for the kids. Dragging this out was not doing them any favors. The sooner they were placed with a family, the sooner their normal childhood could begin.

But Ray and Dorian hated to say goodbye.

"Are you ready to talk to them?" Dorian asked.

Ray stood. "Yeah, I guess."

She stood and called out, "You guys want some brownies? They should be cool enough to eat by now."

The kids cheered and ran toward the door of the cabin. Ray and Dorian took off running too.

"First one there gets the biggest brownie!" Dorian yelled.

He'd never seen two kids run so fast. He wasn't sure he could have beaten them even if he'd truly been trying.

They all stumbled into the house. Ray cut the chocolate goodies while Dorian poured some milk, and they all sat down around the table. It was a tight fit. The table had only been built for two people. He'd had to build a makeshift bench yesterday so all four of them could sit around it.

Savannah immediately began gobbling down her brownie. Theo took his time, savoring. Prime examples of their different personalities.

It took Dorian longer than he'd expected to be able to get the words out. "We need to talk to you guys about your living situation."

Ray's hand slid into his under the table, and he squeezed it before continuing. "Grandfather isn't here, and he isn't coming back. I don't think he meant for you to stay in the hunter's shack through the winter. It will be too cold, and there's not enough animals nearby for you to be able to survive."

Savannah slid a little closer to Theo. Theo had stopped eating his brownie altogether, and color was draining from his face.

Shit. Dorian knew this talk had to happen. But *shit*.

"Dorian and I want to help you," Ray said softly. "We can see about getting you back to Ukraine if that's what you want. Make sure someone can take care of you there."

It didn't take much to see that the kids were highly upset at that idea. Sending them back there wouldn't be Dorian's first choice either.

"Or we can help you find what's called a foster family here in America. Someone to be your American parents," Dorian said.

Theo bit his lip. "But what about . . ." He held out his hand in front of him, waving at nothing. ". . . about not telling anyone."

Dorian nodded, then reached across the table and slid Theo's brownie a little closer to him. "We would make sure you had papers and a story in place that would keep you safe. No one would know who you were or how to find you. We would make sure you have a good family to live with."

"Can we stay with you?" Savannah asked in a tiny voice.

He looked over at Ray, waiting for her to say no.

She didn't.

It was the one thing they hadn't really discussed. Almost like both of them had been unsure of how to broach the topic.

"Do you mean stay with us until we find you a proper family?" Dorian finally asked. "One in a town where there are other kids so you could have friends?"

"Could you be our goster family?" Savannah asked.

"Foster," Ray murmured. Then made the *fos* sound for Savannah to mimic. She still had trouble with certain English sounds.

"Could we stay with you?" Theo asked. "I could help out here. We can clean. I could hunt. We will——"

Dorian reached across the small table and squeezed the boy's hand to stop him. "It's not about your usefulness. We both know how capable and hardworking you are."

"Is it about money? Perhaps you could pay me a wage, and I could pay it back to you . . ."

He looked over at Ray and found her huge blue eyes swimming with tears. Hell, he could feel them burning at the back of his own throat.

"Theo, it's not about you or Savannah or your value. Ray and I have never been parents. We're . . ."

Dorian trailed off, not sure how to continue. How did you explain that both of them suffered from different forms of PTSD? That both of them had been killers? That both of them had blood on their hands that sometimes seemed like it would never wash off?

"We're not sure we know how to be good parents," Ray finished for Dorian. "It's not that we don't want you here, but you deserve to have good parents."

They all sat in silence looking at each other. It was Savannah who finally broke it.

"We'll teach you." She shrugged her small shoulders. "We'll all learn together."

Was it really that simple?

He looked over at Ray. The bemused, hopeful look on her face told him all he needed to know about how she was feeling.

"It would mean changes," he said to her. "Expanding this place. Going partially back on the grid."

After all, Ray was legally dead. And these kids didn't have any legal papers whatsoever.

She nodded. "We'll get Kendrick and Neo on it. You know they can create a paper trail and documents that are airtight."

"Are you sure?"

She smiled. "I thought the choices I made years ago meant that you and I would never get to have a family. Maybe I was wrong."

Dorian looked back at the kids. "Are you sure this is what you want? There are other options. Good options."

Theo nodded so solemnly. "We want to stay with you. Grandfather would've wanted us to stay with you. You will keep us safe."

Dorian nodded at the boy. "We will keep you safe."

"Then I guess you guys are staying," Ray said. "This calls for more brownies."

Everyone cheered. Dorian grabbed her hand as she stood, bringing her palm to his lips, kissing it.

He and Ray had woken up this morning as a family of two. They went to bed that night as a family of four.

Chapter 23

Kendrick spent two days taking care of Neo before she was able to move on her own. Varela's goon had known exactly what he was doing. She had no broken bones, no internal injuries, and if she was fully dressed, someone would be hard-pressed to realize she was injured at all.

But she'd been in a shit ton of pain.

The next morning after he'd brought her to his house, she couldn't walk at all. She'd refused Kendrick's insistence to get some stronger pain meds. Said she wanted to keep her brain clear.

He'd moved her onto the couch in his office so he could work using his whole system and she could utilize both her laptop and the second one he'd provided.

Every twelve hours, they made sure they had something for her to report to Varela. Usually some mix of twenty percent truth and eighty percent lie—but always very convincing. He was demanding the location of Dr. Sevier soon. They wouldn't be able to hold him off on that much longer.

Neo still hadn't told Kendrick exactly what Varela was

holding over her to get her to do his dirty work. But she'd slipped once in a moment of panic, saying how she was afraid Varela would hurt them.

Them. He'd known she wasn't talking about her and him. It could be family, although she'd never mentioned anyone. She'd grown up in foster care and had never mentioned any specific ties.

Had she found her biological parents and Varela was threatening them? Or someone she'd known in the foster system.

Or maybe her favorite third grade teacher's family—Kendrick honestly had no idea.

Varela kept pushing for info on Dr. Sevier's whereabouts. Evidently, Mosaic was pretty hard up for him to finish the work he'd started for them.

If Kendrick and Neo could just find him, they could let him know they were on his side. Work with him to use whatever was on the drive to take down Mosaic and keep the doctor safe.

Because unless they could find him, or get direct access to a Mosaic computer terminal again, this drive wasn't getting cracked anytime soon without corrupting the data. All other methods they wanted to try put the data at risk.

Neo was getting more and more frantic. She was trying to hide it, but Kendrick could see it in her tight shoulders, the way she flinched at the slightest noise, her hands cold in his whenever he touched them.

He held her in his arms when they rested, trying to encourage her to sleep so her body would heal. She did a little—he could feel when her body finally gave in and dropped into a fitful slumber. But it was never enough.

Kendrick sat beside Neo as she sent Varela the latest agreed-upon update. They kept it as vague as possible: they were still hacking traffic cameras to follow Sevier from Salt

Lake City. He'd gone north, and they'd provide more details soon. Hacking this many cameras took time.

It was all the truth.

But Varela was getting impatient. As made clear by his response.

Do I need to demonstrate how serious I am about finding Dr. Sevier? Stop stalling.

Neo wrapped her arms around herself, almost doubling over, breaths so choppy he was afraid she was going to pass out. Kendrick rubbed her shoulder, but it didn't calm her at all.

He didn't know how to calm her, not with Varela's guillotine hanging over her head.

"Neo, it's okay. I know we don't want to give him Dr. Sevier, but we'll work with Ian, get his resources in on this too. Let Varela find Sevier, then Zodiac can rescue him."

"But we don't know where he is."

That was true. They'd been utilizing every camera they'd been able to access—writing programs to search through the footage of the man and look for the car Sevier had been driving.

Like they'd told Varela, he'd gone north. Maybe trying to make it to the Canadian border. But they'd lost him outside of Idaho Falls. Hell, that was only an hour from here. Maybe they'd have a better chance scouring the city themselves.

"I have to tell him something, Kendrick. I have to." She was staring at the phone like it was a bomb in her hands. One they had no way of stopping.

Maybe it was time to stop trying to find Dr. Sevier altogether. They needed to work the *real* problem.

The problem wasn't Sevier. It was *Varela*.

He took the phone from her fingers, and shot back a text. *I'll have a location for you in twelve hours. I swear.*

Kendrick spun the phone around and showed her what

he'd sent. The last of the color leeched from her face and she began shaking.

He scooped her up, ignoring his own discomfort and careful not to cause her undue pain, and placed her in his lap. She wrapped her arms around her knees but didn't pull away from him.

"It's time for us to fight Varela head-on," he said against her hair. "Fight him at his level. If we can't give him what he wants, then we need to stop him from being able to control you. We've got to work the problem."

For the first time, there was a flicker of hope in her eyes.

Kendrick muttered a curse as his phone chimed. The mere sound of a text coming in had her stiffening in his arms.

"Forget it," he told her. "Whoever it is can wait."

She shook her head. "No. You need to get it. It could be important."

It was a text from Dorian. *Need emergency computer help here. ASAP.*

He let out a curse.

"What?"

He showed her the text. "Dorian and Ray don't mess around with terms like *emergency* and *ASAP*. If they want me, it's not to set up their wireless printer."

Kendrick shot back a text. *Anything I can work on from here? Need to give details f2f only. TS.*

From anyone else TS—top secret—and face-to-face only would seem melodramatic. Not from Dorian and Ray.

But it didn't matter. Kendrick had to handle one crisis at a time. And the woman in his arms took priority. He pulled her closer. "Dorian and Ray can wait. You are my focus right now, my only concern."

She peeked up at him. "I don't deserve you."

He trailed a finger down her cheek, hating that she

flinched. "You deserve so much more than you give yourself credit for. So much more than you allow yourself to accept."

"But I—"

"—made shitty choices but for understandable reasons. The important thing is we're not going to give Varela any more reasons to work with. We stop it—stop *him*. Whatever we need to do."

Kendrick didn't look over when his phone pinged again. He wanted her to know she had his undivided attention. Dorian would eventually show up at his house if Kendrick kept ignoring him, but he'd deal with the big man later.

Right now . . . her.

But Neo had other plans. "Let's go help Dorian and Ray —neither of us is going to be able to concentrate until we do. Then I'll tell you everything."

He kissed her. *Now* they were working the problem.

Chapter 24

The last thing Kendrick expected to see when he finally found Ray and Dorian's cabin—finding it during the day wasn't much easier than at night—were two kids with them.

Not just *with* them. Playing and laughing with them.

"Ray and Dorian have kids?" Neo asked. "I had no idea."

"They didn't the last time I saw them, which was a few days ago."

Kendrick shook hands with Dorian. The big man and Neo nodded at each other but kept their distance.

Kendrick could barely keep his eyes off Ray. He'd known the woman for years now but had never seen her like this. She was beaming as she and the little boy and girl played some version of monkey in the middle with a pinecone.

"It's hard to argue that motherhood doesn't suit her, seeing her like this, isn't it?" Dorian said as they watched Ray tuck a strand of hair behind the little girl's ear before saying something with a laugh.

"Motherhood?" Kendrick asked. "These kids weren't hiding in a closet when I was here last week, right?"

"No. They've been living in a hunter's shack for two weeks. Came to stay with us a couple of days ago."

Dorian took them inside and explained what they needed to know. Someone had killed the kids' grandfather and they were in danger. Plus, they were illegal aliens without any sort of paperwork.

"We offered to make sure they could have a good, safe life there, but they don't want to go back to Ukraine. We offered to help get them set up with a more traditional family —get them papers and put them in the foster system."

"They didn't want that either?" Kendrick asked.

"They want to stay with us. And . . ." The big man shrugged, a bemused look on his face. "I can't really explain it. We want them to stay with us too."

"You just knew?" Neo asked. Kendrick expected to find skepticism littering her features, but she was staring at Dorian intently.

The big man shrugged again. "I know it sounds crazy, but Ray and I both just knew. These are our kids. They're ours."

"Just like that," she said.

It wasn't a question; it was an agreement. A sentimental one, at that. Not what he expected from Neo.

"I guess it sounds crazy to you," Dorian said.

Neo shook her head. "No. Not at all. It sounds beautiful. Perfect."

Dorian shrugged. "Not all families are formed in the traditional way."

"But they're still family," Neo whispered.

What was going on in her brain? She definitely seemed to have a better grip on this new family of Dorian and Ray's than he did.

"So you need us to work up some papers for them, right?" he asked.

Dorian nodded. "That, and airtight adoption paperwork. IDs for Ray and me. We're going to go back on the grid, so there can't be any connection to our former lives."

Holy hell. Dorian and Ray had spent the past two years and untold amounts of money making sure they weren't on the grid *at all*. That's what this secret Batcave was all about—being able to live here without there being any record of them.

Kendrick scrubbed a hand down his face. "D, man, are you sure? This is going to change everything."

"I've never been more sure of anything in my life. But I'm trusting you with the most important things in the world to me. Airtight, Blaze. These IDs and backgrounds cannot be cracked."

It was Neo who answered. "Between the two of us, we will make sure there is no way anyone will ever be able to hurt your family electronically. No one will ever connect the people you've become to the people you were when I first met you. I will personally build in failsafe that will never be hacked."

Kendrick had never seen Neo so dedicated. But no one could mistake the sincerity in her voice.

He stepped up next to her and squeezed her shoulder. "It'll take a few days for us to build it. You'll want it done right from the beginning. So unless you need to flee the country in the next twenty-four hours, let us take time to formulate the proper layers."

Dorian nodded. "Okay. We're going to want to eventually get them into school, but for right now, they'll be staying here in this cabin. No one will be around."

"Okay. Neo and I have a situation of our own we have to deal with—one that we might be calling in everyone to help with. But as soon as that's done, we'll get you the papers and background you need.

Kendrick pulled out his computer and Neo pulled out hers. They sat at the kitchen table.

"Let's go ahead and get some basics down," Kendrick said. "Their ages and preferences for names."

"And if you and Ray have any preferences for names too," Neo added.

"We want to stay around here. It's going to be more important than ever to have family around us. We want the kids to grow up with Ethan and Jess and any other Linear kids . . ."

"So you'll need to remain as you," Kendrick finish for him. "Too many people around Oak Creek know you."

Dorian nodded. "The only people who know Ray are related to Linear. So she'll need a new name and ID—anyone but Grace Brandt."

Kendrick nodded over at Neo. "Probably will be easiest to build the kids as Ray's biological children who came into your family when you married her. You adopted them, it's now finalized, and they live with you guys."

Neo agreed. "Give people a boring story and they'll never think twice about it. Stepkids are common."

Dorian filled them in on the details, and they began building profiles. They weren't far into it when Ray and the kids came inside.

"It's time to make banana bread!" The little girl was holding Ray's hand.

"You must be Savannah." Neo smiled at her. "You like to bake?"

"I'm better than Ray at banana bread," Savannah whispered loudly.

"Yeah." Ray ruffled her hair. "But I make the best brownies."

Kendrick turned to the boy. "And you must be Theo. It's nice to meet—"

"Why do you have grandfather's picture?" Theo pointed at Kendrick's computer screen. It had switched to the screen-saver that he'd made from the picture of Dr. Sevier.

All the adults in the room froze.

Neo pointed to the screen. "That is your grandfather?"

"Are you bad?" Theo looked from Kendrick to Dorian. "Are these the bad people?"

Dorian squatted down next to the boy. "No. I promise you, these are our friends. They didn't hurt your grandfather. They're trying to figure out who did."

Not exactly, but close enough. Kendrick caught Neo's eye.

The kids' grandfather was dead. *Dr. Sevier* was dead. That changed the entire game.

Kendrick reached into his bag and pulled out the drive he'd brought with them. "Do you know anything about this? It was your grandfather's."

Theo's face fell once again. He turned to Dorian. "That was what he gave away the night I stayed at the hotel and he got hurt."

Dorian put a hand on the boy's shoulder. "Still not your fault. Your grandfather risked his life getting that drive to the right people. Then he got you here because you two are just as important."

Ray stepped closer, putting her arm around Theo and Savannah. "Kendrick and Neo are going to help us be a family, get us the papers we need. They're also trying to catch the people who hurt Grandfather. They're our friends and yours too."

Kendrick and Neo both smiled at the kids, although they both still looked nervous.

Ray grabbed both their hands. "Let's go back out and play for a little bit, okay? We'll make banana bread tonight." The kids went with her without a word.

Both Kendrick and Neo slumped back in their chairs.

"Sevier is dead," Neo whispered. "I spent all this time trying to find him, sabotaging everything . . ."

Kendrick grabbed her hand. "It's okay. This gives us more to use against Varela."

Dorian studied them but didn't ask any questions.

"Mosaic's pit bull has been gunning for Dr. Sevier, a.k.a. Grandfather, pretty damned hard," Kendrick explained. "Neo got caught in the middle of it, but we've spent the past two days feeding Mosaic mostly false info about him. Trying to reach him before they did."

"Was Sevier working for Mosaic?"

"He was being forced to." Kendrick looked pointedly over at Neo as he said it. She needed to accept that she wasn't the only one Mosaic had coerced. "But he wanted out. He contacted Ian DeRose but then dropped off the grid before Ian could work out a plan."

Dorian rubbed the back of his neck. "He was trying to get the kids here to the States with him. They would've been alone back in Ukraine. Parents dead."

"Evidently, he hid part of his research, plus info about Mosaic, on the drive. Tried to create some sort of insurance for himself."

"What do you need to open it?" Dorian asked. "You've been trying for over a week."

"That was my fault." Neo's voice was tight. "We need the code, plus we discovered the drive has a DNA-scan failsafe. We need Dr. Sevier's DNA."

"Can you get it off a dead body?" Dorian asked.

Kendrick glanced at Neo, then back to Dorian. "Gross, but yes. Do you have his dead body?"

"The kids buried him, but we know where. Probably needs to be re-dug deeper anyway. Might give kids more closure to do a ceremony or something."

Kendrick rubbed the back of his neck. "Have the kids mentioned any codes? We're looking for fifteen digits, alphanumeric. Maybe Sevier put it in their belongings?"

Dorian nodded. "They had some books. Let me get them."

The three of them pored over the children's books but found nothing written inside, nothing underlined or highlighted in any way.

"Can we take these with us?" Neo asked. "It won't take much effort to build a program that searches the books for patterns."

"Sure." Dorian stood. "Let me go ask the kids if their grandfather taught them any codes. It might be best if I talk to them alone."

Kendrick nodded. Theo trusted Dorian, not them.

He and Neo sat there looking at each other, both of their brains processing all the new developments. But where Kendrick was feeling more hopeful about what was ahead of them, Neo obviously was not.

He could recognize the withdrawal signals. And goddammit, he wasn't going to allow it. This was not her problem to solve alone. "Whatever you're thinking you can stop it right fucking now."

"We were willing to sacrifice Dr. Sevier to buy me time with Varela."

He shrugged. "I feel bad that he's dead, and I hate it for those kids, but his death—especially since we can access his DNA—makes our lives easier. As long as Mosaic doesn't know he's dead, it works in our favor."

"But they're going to figure it out. It was one thing to be willing to sacrifice Dr. Sevier. I can't sacrifice Savannah and Theo."

"We won't."

She brought both hands up to her forehead and rubbed

the skin there over and over. "That's what we want to believe. But we can't know that for sure."

It didn't even sound like she was talking to him. She was talking to herself.

"We will keep those kids safe, Neo."

"There's only one way to know for sure. Only one."

He wanted to stop the frantic movement of her hands but was afraid to touch her. He'd never seen her like this. "How? How do we know for sure?"

"Take me out of the equation."

"How? By telling Varela to fuck off?" Kendrick was one hundred percent in support of that plan.

"No." She stopped rubbing her head, lowered her hands to her lap like she'd accepted the finality of her plan. "Take me out of the equation *permanently*. I was going to do it the other night before you showed up at my house, but I was too chicken. But I'm ready now. I'll do it right in front of Varela. This is the only way to be sure."

She was talking about killing herself.

It took every ounce of willpower Kendrick had not to leap across the table and shake her until her teeth rattled. No way. No *fucking way* was he entertaining this line of thinking even for a second.

"It's the only way to be sure," she repeated.

He could appreciate that she was willing to dive on this grenade, but . . . no. He walked over and crouched down beside her.

"I'm not losing those kids. But I'm not losing you either, Neoma. Not a chance in hell." When he did touch her, his hands were gentle. He picked her hand up and brought her palm to his lips. She needed gentle now more than ever. "And whoever it is Varela is threatening? We're not losing them either."

She started to respond but Dorian walked back into the kitchen. "Um . . . everything okay?"

"Yeah. Neo and I were making sure the bottom line was clear. Did you find out anything?"

"Nothing. They can't remember any series of letters or numbers their grandfather told them to remember."

Damn it. "Okay."

"I'll go back over to the shack they were in and search there. Ray will go through all their clothes and personal items. If they have it, we'll find it."

"D, we've spent a lot of time researching Dr. Sevier." Neo flinched and he stroked his thumb against the back of her hand. He got up so he could face Dorian but didn't stop touching her.

"Mosaic isn't far behind us when it comes to the drive. It won't take long for them to piece together that Sevier was traveling with two kids. They'll be coming for Theo and Savannah. Until we crack that drive, those kids are definitely in danger, even here with you."

Dorian crossed his arms over his massive chest. "Ray and I aren't going to let anything happen to them. They're ours now."

It was impossible to doubt his sincerity.

"Agreed." Kendrick nodded. "And the DNA might give us something new to work with until we find the code, or find a way around it."

"Theo and Savannah's safety is the most important thing."

"Yes it is." Neo stood now too.

He wrapped his arm around her. "So is yours, don't you forget that." He looked back at Dorian. "This is bigger than what we can handle alone. It's time to call in everyone. We need all hands on deck. Right now."

Chapter 25

Bring me the drive or they die.

The picture attached to the text made Neo want to vomit. It took every bit of self-control she had not to leave her perch against the back wall and sneak out the door while no one was looking.

She'd promised not to do anything rash on her own. And even if she hadn't, Kendrick had gone all hawk-eyed on her. If she left now, he'd be on her heels a second after. He hadn't let her out of his sight for a minute—had literally stood outside the bathroom door when she'd gone—since their talk at Ray and Dorian's place a couple hours ago.

There hadn't been a chance for them to talk further. She needed to explain to him exactly what was going on, but first they had to make sure Theo and Savannah were safe. She should've had another eight hours to figure out what to do about the other.

But Varela had upped the timeline a few minutes ago. She gripped the phone with shaking hands. Just breathing hurt. Like she had a cement block sitting on her chest slowly crushing her.

She looked around from her perch at the back of the large Linear Tactical training facility—trying to think, not panic.

She'd been at this place many times, had actually done some of the indoor training here the Linear guys were known for. SWAT teams and law enforcement groups came from all over the country to train with them.

This place was permeated with memories for the LT family. She hadn't known them then, but Finn and Charlie had had their wedding reception here. Jordan Reiss-Collingwood had made her peace with the town here.

But Anne Mackay had almost been killed by a psychopath here too. So, good and bad memories.

They were here now because it was the only building big enough to hold all of them. And it was *all* of them. She wasn't sure she'd ever seen the entire Linear Tactical team in one place before.

All the main guys, the ones who had started or currently worked for the company—Zac, Finn, Aiden, Gavin, Wyatt, Heath, Dorian.

Some of them were talking to each other, some were standing close to their wives. Even the guys not directly employed by Linear were here—Baby, Boy Riley, Cade O'Conner, Gabe Collingwood, Ian DeRose.

It was impressive on so many different levels. Whether they were former Special Forces soldiers or not, all of these men were capable of handling damn near any crisis that came their way.

Just as admirable were the women in the building. All unique, but each an integral part of the strength of the men who loved them.

After a year of seeing some of these couples interact with each other, the most impressive thing Neo had noticed was the respect the men and women had for each other. They might bicker, they might joke—for the rest of her life Neo would smile at the obnoxiously named drinks Lexi still served Gavin at the Eagle's Nest—but the bonds between each of these couples were unbreakable.

Short of death, nothing was ever going to tear them apart. Not the individual couples and not the family as a whole.

All it had taken to get everyone to drop everything and show up here on an early Sunday morning had been a call from Dorian saying he needed them.

It could've been a call from any of them—had been in the past—and they all would've shown up.

Because that's what family did. They showed up for each other.

Neo had never had that. She looked down at the image on her phone and Varela's text. Her chest tightened more.

She needed it now. Needed what this group of friends was offering Dorian and Ray: their unconditional support.

She had no right to ask for it. She didn't know how to ask for it. Didn't know if she should dare try.

Dorian lifted a hand to get everyone's attention. "So, you guys probably missed the memo, but Ray's and my family has doubled since you last saw us."

All the separate conversations stopped. His sentence was punctuated by the sound of laughing children on the small swing set outside the propped-open doors. Theo and Savannah were busy playing with Jess and Ethan. The four of them had immediately gelled together the way only kids could do.

"We recently found out that Savannah and Theo's deceased guardian was a Dr. Claude Sevier," Dorian continued. "Dr. Sevier was being coerced by Mosaic to help them develop mind-altering methods of human trafficking via neuromorphic engineering."

"What they'd hoped to try on Lexi, right?" Gavin slipped an arm around his fiancée, pulling her close. Wyatt's fiancée, Nadine, stood on the other side of her. Evidently, those two had become friends despite a difficult past together.

"Probably." It was Ian DeRose who spoke up now. He had the most information on Mosaic. Dorian gestured for Ian to continue.

"As best we can tell, Mosaic was planning to take Dr. Sevier from his labs in Europe and force him to finish his research in their labs—so they could use it for whatever they wanted. Dr. Sevier copied not only his work, but all the details he could find about Mosaic itself and put it on the drive. We think he was going to use it to ensure Theo and Savannah's safety. He tried to run with them but was shot in the process and died."

Neo turned to watch the children play through the cracked door as Ian continued explaining about Dr. Sevier and how multiple people had been hurt or killed getting the drive to them. She wasn't sure if she fit in that category or not.

Dorian resumed talking about how Mosaic would be coming after the kids. Immediately a combined murmur filled the room.

These men, these women . . . they weren't going to let that happen. If Mosaic wanted Theo and Savannah, it would have to be through them first. A united front.

Her phone buzzed in her hand again and a cold sweat broke out all over her body.

I feel like I don't adequately have your attention, Neo.

Another picture. This time Porter was standing right outside the house. So close she could see into the front windows.

She knew the house, had spent hours looking into those

same windows over the years, although she'd never been inside.

I'm waiting for a response, Neo. What happens next is up to you.

Theo and Savannah were laughing outside once again. Little Jess was bossing everyone around like soldiers even though she was the youngest, and they were all singing something. So happy. So innocent.

Dorian had his arm around Ray, a shared smile between them as they also heard the kids.

She pushed herself off the wall and spoke before she could think through all the ramifications of what would happen if they said no.

"I need protection too."

Everyone turned to stare at her. She had no idea who knew what she'd done. If they did, they'd have every right to turn their backs on her.

"We're not going to let them hurt you." Kendrick walked over to stand beside her.

She shook her head, looking up at him but speaking loud enough for everyone to hear. "It's not for me. It's for the daughter I placed for adoption ten years ago. Varela knows about her and her adoptive family. He's sent somebody there to hurt them." Her voice was getting more frantic, but she couldn't help it. "If I don't get him the drive and all the info about Dr. Sevier, he's going to—"

She couldn't finish. Could barely stay upright. A scream was building up inside her that couldn't be released. This was all her fault. Her fault.

The daughter she'd given up so she'd never be hurt was now about to be killed because of her.

Kendrick's arms wrapped around her, supported her, kept her from flying into the million pieces she could feel herself breaking into.

"Maggie," she sobbed. "They named her Maggie."

The thought of Maggie or the people she called Mommy and Daddy being hurt because of her sliced through her in agonizing waves.

She grabbed Kendrick's shirt, shoved the picture of Porter in Kendrick's face. "Please. You don't have to help me. But help them. They're innocent. They having nothing to do with this."

Kendrick let out a curse, then yanked her against his chest. "Neo, of course. Of course we will."

She couldn't bear to look around. Couldn't breathe. Everyone else might feel differently. She wasn't a part of this family.

"Your daughter. Her family. Where do they live?" Ian asked.

"Denver. Varela has a man there now. If I don't report . . ." The pain nearly doubled her over again. Kendrick pulled her tighter against him.

There was talk going on around her but she couldn't hear it over the roaring in her ears. She'd been so helpless as a child—she'd fought her entire adult life to never, ever feel that way again.

But she was helpless now. She couldn't keep everyone safe no matter what she did.

There was only one way to be sure. They were back to that. "I have to—"

Kendrick kissed her.

"Stop, Neoma." He murmured against her lips. "For once, lean on someone else. We can help."

"But I—"

"Listen to what they're saying."

He pulled back, then placed her in front of him, easing his arms around her so her back was resting against his chest.

The people surrounding her were talking about how to help.

Ian looked over at Gabe. She knew the two men had served in the Navy SEALs together. "We need to eliminate the threat against Neo immediately. Take the jet?"

Gabe gave him a nod. "Consider it handled." He raised his chin at Aiden. "You up for a field trip?"

"I'm coming too," Violet, Aiden's wife and Gabe's sister, interjected. "And don't you dare give me the stink eye, big brother. I spend just as much time in the gym, in the ring, and on the shooting range as you do."

Everybody in the room smiled. Neo hadn't known Violet before she'd been kidnapped—the reason that had brought Kendrick to Oak Creek to begin with. But there was no doubt the redhead was a complete badass now, as well as a phenomenal baker.

"We'd be glad to have you at our back, little sis." Gabe said, wrapping an arm around her. He looked over at Neo with a nod. "No one will hurt your daughter or her family."

Neo blinked. That was it? She mentioned that she had trouble and a billionaire security company owner was sending his former Navy SEAL buddy to go handle it in his private jet?

What if they found out the truth once they got to Denver and decided not to help after all?

She tried to step away from Kendrick but he wouldn't let go.

"I'm the reason Kendrick didn't crack the drive before now." She looked at Ian, then over to Gabe, Violet, and Aiden.

"You, plus needing the DNA of someone we couldn't find, not to mention a fifteen-digit alphanumeric code." Kendrick shook his head. "Even if you'd been helping me, we wouldn't have been able to crack it."

This time she used more effort to pull away. Kendrick

was too close to her, literally and figuratively. His emotions were involved when it came to her. He wasn't neutral.

She looked around at everyone else. "I had surveillance set up in your homes when I first arrived in town. I turned the equipment off after couple weeks, but I never took it out."

"We know," Annie said softly.

"Hell." Charlie rolled her eyes. "Finn used that as an excuse to have sex in the living room with me five times before we found out you turned it off. He figured if you wanted a show, he'd give you one."

"What?" She spun around to look at Kendrick.

"They all knew." He shrugged. "We had a whole meeting about it back when we first found out."

She turned around slowly, her chest heavy once again. "You knew all along but didn't tell me? Let me think I was your friend?"

She had no right to feel betrayed here, but she would've rather had them run her out of town at the beginning than string her along for the past year.

Zac stepped forward, always the leader. "You were close to Kendrick, so we talked with him. He immediately rerouted the transmissions so you were getting useless feedback. Although we're all happy to hear that Finn got extra lucky that week."

She couldn't joke about this. "I never listened, not even once. I promise. I just . . . I didn't know how to trust people."

Ray walked over and squeezed her shoulder. "If you're going to claim that, you'll have to get in line behind me. Maybe Dorian can tell you the story of the time I shot him with my crossbow."

"Or Ray could tell you how I dragged her to an abandoned cabin and threatened to torture her," Dorian shot back.

Lexi raised her hand from the back of the room. "I pretended to be someone else for months."

Shy Peyton O'Conner waved. "Didn't tell anyone who the father of my child was for years."

Baby saluted with a grin. "Failed to mention I couldn't read for three decades."

"Refused to let anyone know I had MS!" Girl Riley yelled from the far side of the room.

"Still salty about that," Boy Riley responded from next to her and everyone chuckled.

"Didn't see fit to let anyone know I was homeless and living out of my car." Charlie winked at Neo on the other side of Kendrick, a wiggling baby Thomas trying to get down from her arms.

Ray smiled. "See? You're not the only one who has struggled with trust."

Ian walked forward. "You didn't know how to trust then. But trust us now. We're not going to let anything happen to the people you care about." He turned to Dorian and Ray. "Those kids of yours either."

"We'll keep them safe, however long it takes," Zac said.

Everyone around her nodded. Repeats of "however long it takes" echoed through the building.

"Thank you." It was all she could say. Kendrick's arms slipped around her.

"We're family," Zac said, pulling Anne close. "And like it or not, you're part of us now. This family looks out for one another."

Chapter 26

For the first time since this had begun, Kendrick felt like he was playing the game with all the pieces. No more running blind, no more hands tied behind his back.

Within minutes of Neo accepting their help, Gabe, Aiden, and Violet had Maggie's address and were on their way to Denver in the Zodiac Tactical jet. Wyatt had decided to go along with them in case the situation proved more complicated.

Maggie.

Of all the secrets he'd thought Neo might be keeping, her having placed a daughter for adoption as a teenager wasn't one that had ever crossed his mind.

"We need to figure out what you should tell Varela."

They'd already told him to stop with the scare tactics so she could work if he wanted results. Varela had respected the show of bravado, but they both knew the time it had bought was limited.

Zac, along with Baby and Boy Riley, had taken Anne and left to do the unpleasant but needed work of gathering Dr. Sevier's DNA.

The others were working together to devise the best method of protecting Theo and Savannah.

Neo had been tasked with turning the tables on Varela. If he could use what he'd found about her against her, then maybe the same could be done to him. It's what they would've already done if she'd come to him from the beginning. Worked all angles of the problem.

Besides, his little loner seemed like she needed something to do. The show of solidarity for her, while appreciated, had been a little overwhelming for someone used to battling her demons on her own.

Meanwhile, until Zac and Annie got back with the DNA, Kendrick was starting to build the paperwork and electronic background for Theo and Savannah. The sooner they were fully in the system, the less likely Mosaic was to look their way.

Once they had the DNA, they'd try to work around the fifteen-digit code without destroying the contents of the drive. It was a long shot, but at this point they'd take advantage of anything they could.

A few minutes later, little Jess came running inside, zigzagging through the adults until she found her mom and dad, who were talking to Gavin and Lexi.

"Mom! Mom!"

Peyton raised an eyebrow at her daughter. Jess fell silent before muttering, "Excuse me, may I interrupt momentarily?"

Everyone swallowed a snicker over the line that had obviously been rehearsed with Jess more than once.

"Yes, Jess. How can I help you?" Peyton said.

"Mom! I have a new friend, and her name is Savannah, and Uncle Dorian and Aunt Ray are her mom and dad." All Jess's words came out in a rush, like they always tended to.

"Evidently, that's a complicated story. I'm still trying to work out the details."

More swallowed snickers. Especially as Jess side-eyed Dorian like she was trying to figure out if he'd always had these two kids and had left Jess out of the loop.

Leaving her out of the loop was a nearly unpardonable sin in the six-year-old's eyes.

"Yes, we've met Theo and Savannah, Uncle Dorian and Aunt Ray's new children," Peyton responded serenely. "Do you have an actual question?"

The little girl nodded. "Savannah has never ever had a sleepover. *Ever*, Mom."

It wasn't hard to see where this was going.

"Jess." Peyton let out a sigh. "I'm not sure now is the right time to invite Savannah for a sleepover . . ."

"Actually." Cade slid an arm around his wife while looking over at Ray and Dorian. "Our house might be the perfect place for security until this is all settled. We're already set up for kids. Our place is big enough to give everyone their own space. I've got heightened security and guards."

Cade had almost lost Peyton and Jess once because of his country music super-star status. The man wasn't going to take a chance on that happening again. Someone of his wealth and fame attracted the crazies. Cade had made sure his family was safe.

"Of course. And we would love to have you and the kids around to hang out with," Peyton said to Ray. "Or we could give you as much space and privacy as you want. Like Cade said, there's plenty of room."

Ray and Dorian did that thing where they communicated with each other without ever speaking.

Then Dorian nodded. "That would be great, thank you. We're not sure how long this is going to drag out, but we'd like to make everything as stress-free for the kids as we can."

"That means yes!" Jess yelled. "We can divide my room in half if Savannah wants to stay in there. We would each have eight by nine and a half feet to ourselves. That's twelve point two percent smaller than the average bedroom size in the average North American home. I don't think social services will have any problem with us sharing since it's temporary."

They all shook their head at their little resident genius. Neither the fact that she could do the math in her head nor that she knew the average bedroom size in North America surprised anyone.

"Why don't you go tell Theo and Savannah they're going to stay with us for a while, smarty-pants? Cade ruffled his daughter's hair. "Be sure to mention Aunt Ray and Uncle Dorian will be staying too so they're not worried."

"Poor Ethan." Jess let out a huge sigh, eyes getting wide. "He's going to be so sad that he's getting left out of all the fun."

Kendrick had to swallow a bark of laughter at Jess's obvious attempt to manipulate her father. When it came to Ethan, Jess would do nearly anything to keep him near her.

Cade crossed his arms over his chest. "Nope, not a chance. But he can come over for pancakes in the morning."

Jess obviously knew when to cut her losses. She smiled and nodded, then skipped back out the door, singing some crazy song.

It was Lyn Zimmerman-Kavanaugh, Gavin's sister, who was only here for a few more weeks before she and her husband Heath left for her new job in Egypt, who stopped Jess. "Hey, what song is that you're singing?"

"Savannah taught it to me. She told me she would teach me some words in Ukrainian. I already know how to speak French and Spanish, but not Ukrainian." Her eyes lit up. "I like to learn new things."

They were all very aware of that.

"Can you sing it for me again?" Lyn asked. She looked over at Heath. "My Ukrainian is rusty."

"Mine too. But . . ."

"*Che sim sim odyn, ju yee sist ju. Try em odyn. Sist che che sim.*" Everyone winced as Jess sang the ditty again. She might be a child prodigy but it definitely wasn't due to her vocal skills.

"The kids sing that all the time," Dorian said. "They said it's nonsense."

"It does sound like gibberish, but . . ." Lyn turned to Heath. "Did you get that?"

He nodded. "*Che*, seven, seven, one. One again twice more toward the end."

Kendrick slid back from his computer. "*Odyn* means one?" He'd heard that very clearly, like Odin from the *Thor* movies. Jess had said it distinctly three times.

Heath nodded. "Yes. And *sim* is seven."

"What is *che*?" he asked.

"It's a letter used in Slavic languages, in the Cyrillic alphabet. We don't have an equivalent in English." Lyn had recently finished her dissertation in linguistics, so she knew what she was talking about. "Does somebody have a pen? I'll show you what it looks like."

They had five numbers and a letter. And more sounds in the ditty that hadn't been translated.

Maybe there were fifteen.

Kendrick looked over at Neo to find her watching him, getting up from her computer. She was thinking the same thing he was.

Ray walked over to the door and yelled for Theo and Savannah to come in. She'd realized what they were thinking too.

It didn't take them long to have the words of the tune translated.

Che. Seven. Seven. One. *Yu. Yee.* Six. *Yu.* Three. M. One. Six. *Che. Che.* One.

The numbers were easy. The letter M was similar in both languages. Lyn drew the other Cyrillic letters, *che* and *yu*, with the help of Theo and Savannah.

"See?" the boy said. "It doesn't make any sense."

Savannah nodded. "Grandfather said it was silly but that silly is good sometimes."

Ray dropped to a crouch and tweaked Savannah's nose. "He was right. Silly is definitely good."

Kendrick looked over at Neo, unable to keep the smile from his face. "We've got our fifteen-digit alphanumeric code. It was with us the whole time."

Chapter 27

It worked. All it took to open the drive was a made-up nursery rhyme and the strand of a dead man's hair.

As soon as Dr. Anne provided the needed DNA, Neo and Kendrick attached the drive to Kendrick's computer and began the upload process. First the fifteen-digit code, which they never would have been able to crack by brute force or side-channel attack because they'd have been looking in the wrong alphabet.

Once the correct sequence was typed in, a small slot on the drive slid open for DNA, and voila . . . she gave up all her secrets.

Kendrick switched on the screen so they could see the file listings as they downloaded. First files were all security measures. They were impressive. Dr. Sevier had known what he was doing.

"Holy shit," Kendrick said, tapping on the screen as a list scrolled up. "Did you see that?"

Neo had seen it, but it didn't excuse what she'd done. "Doesn't change anything."

"What did you see?" Ian asked.

"I thought I had gotten close to cracking this thing the other night when we were at the travel agency building with some brute-force hacking. But if I had kept going the way that I had, if Neo hadn't pulled the alarm and forced us to leave immediately, I would have triggered a secondary defense protocol and the drive would've corrupted itself." He smiled over at her. "See? It all worked out for the best."

She rolled her eyes. "Yeah, that's why I did it. Because I knew it was all for the best."

Kendrick squeezed her shoulder and they watched more of the data roll in. They could only read the file names and designations, but it was enough to give them an idea.

"You've got a shit ton of scientific stuff here," Kendrick said. "No wonder Mosaic wants this drive so badly. But given the size of these data files, I'm not sure if Sevier had as much on Mosaic itself as we hoped."

Ian leaned a hip on the edge of the table. "It's more than we had. It's enough to launch an offensive."

"We'll keep digging through it to get every possible bit of information we can," Neo said to him. "I'm committed to taking them down."

Ian nodded. "We'll need all the help we can get."

The drive was a little less than halfway downloaded when the phone rang on the table next to her. Varela. She looked around frantically.

"Everybody quiet!" Kendrick yelled.

Cade and Peyton shooed the kids back outside, closing the door behind them. Everyone else in the training facility fell silent. Kendrick nodded at her. And she pressed receive on the call.

"This would go more quickly if you would leave me alone to work." She forced as much bravado into her voice as she could.

"I see you're at the Linear Tactical training facility."

She forced herself not to panic. Kendrick leaned in so he could hear what Varela was saying.

"Yeah, I am. Congratulations on figuring out how to utilize the GPS tracker on this phone. I'm here because this is who Kendrick works with. I'm using every contact I can to squeeze information. I didn't think you'd have a problem with that."

"I don't have a problem with that."

"What do you want, Varela? It's hard to find somewhere private here to talk. I'm in a fucking closet."

"I've given you too much leeway. I don't think you're properly motivated."

She wasn't sure how to counter that, but so far he'd responded best to her being tough. "And I think maybe you've overplayed your hand. Threatening a kid whose life I've never been a part of? I mean, how much could I really care about a child I gave up for adoption?"

Saying the words made her want to vomit. She couldn't stand the thought of Kendrick hearing this. Of what he must think of her. Giving her daughter up for adoption had been anything but abandonment. It had been the best a sixteen-year-old with no home and no family could hope to do.

A hand rubbed the back of her neck. There was no disgust in Kendrick's eyes, just understanding and support.

"I don't think that's the case at all," Varela scoffed. "You were awfully quick to acquiesce once we threatened young Maggie. So you're going to stop stalling and tell me what you know."

She looked at Kendrick, then over at Ian. Both nodded. Kendrick mouthed the words: *Buy time.*

Gabe would be in Denver soon. She had to trust that his team would get to Maggie. The only thing left to tell Varela was the truth.

"Dr. Sevier is dead. I found that out a couple hours ago."

235

Silence. "If this is some sort of wild goose chase . . ."

"It's not. One of your own merry band of idiots shot him. Sevier barely made it out of Salt Lake City."

"How do I know this is not another lie? A misdirect?"

"I found a John Doe that matched Sevier's description in some town. I hacked into their system and got a photo ID confirmation. It was Sevier."

"What town?"

Oh shit.

Kendrick was already typing.

"Jesus, Varela, do you know how much data I'm coming across every hour? I can't keep track of everything off the top of my head. Hold on."

Kendrick spun his computer around and pointed at a town on a map.

"Portage, Utah. I think Sevier was trying to make it to the Canadian border."

Varela was silent for a long minute. Kendrick continued to type, probably hacking into that county's morgue to cover her tracks.

"This changes things," Varela finally said.

"I know. But listen. I'm pretty sure I can crack the drive. Give me about three hours—"

"Take the drive and bring it to me right now."

"Wait. What? I can't. Just give me an hour or two. It will take time—"

"Now."

"But they'll know—"

"I don't care what they know. You have two minutes to walk out the door with the drive in your hand. If not, I guess we'll find out how you really feel about your daughter and her family. Two minutes, Neo. I want a video call from you in your car by yourself with the drive. I'll send you directions then."

The line went dead.

Neo couldn't wrap her head around what she should do. The drive wasn't finished downloading. They didn't have all the information. If Varela somehow got away with it, Mosaic would have all of Dr. Sevier's research.

Could she fake it? How? There wasn't enough time.

There were so many variables. So many scenarios. None of them ended well.

"Before you start talking about killing yourself again, get up and somebody give her keys to a car." Kendrick was already disconnecting the drive and packing up her computer in its backpack.

She looked over at Ian, expecting him to argue, to say she couldn't take the drive with her, but he was pulling out her chair for her. "Go."

"We can't just give Varela the drive."

Kendrick grabbed her by both upper arms and pulled her in, kissing her hard. "Your job right now is to buy time for Gabe and the team to get to Maggie. And to stay alive yourself. We'll be right behind you. Varela thinks you're in this alone. We'll use that against him."

"But . . ." There were so many things that could go wrong.

Kendrick cupped her cheeks. "In the car, Neoma. Trust us."

This time, she kissed him. "I do. With everything."

"Here, take this." Ray put some sort of earpiece in Neo's hand. "Dorian has a transmitter in his watch. We'll be able to hear what's going on with you and communicate."

Neo wasn't sure why Ray had something like this with her, but she'd take it.

"Ray . . ." Dorian said.

Ray held up a hand to stop him. "Neo is risking every-thing too. I'll be all right. I've got you with me, and that's enough. We both know the earpiece is more of a security blanket for me at this point."

Neo didn't know what that meant, but she was out of time. Kendrick grabbed her hand and ran her to a car. She didn't even know whose it was. Someone had given her their vehicle without a word.

"Whatever you need to do," Kendrick said as he opened the door and she got in. "Whatever you need to say—don't hesitate. Just know when the moment of crisis comes, we've got your back."

She had to trust. That was all she could do.

She cranked the car and peeled out of the parking area. Immediately she pressed redial on her phone for a video call.

"I've got it." She held up the drive so Varela could see it. "It's not going to take long for them to figure out I'm gone and that I took it. Where do you want me to go? I don't have much time."

She threw the phone onto the seat so she could grip the steering wheel with both hands.

"I really hope this is not some elaborate ploy on your part, Neoma. There are terrible things that could be done to a ten-year-old girl. Things I don't want to see happen. Things that would be so much crueler than a quick death."

Her hands tightened on the wheel until her knuckles turned white. "Goddammit, I've done what you asked. Leave them alone."

"We'll see. Meet me at the burned warehouse off Route 138. You've got ten minutes."

The line went dead. Arguing that it would take at least fifteen minutes to get to that location wouldn't change the end result.

He was looking for a reason to hurt Maggie and her family.

"Gavin says cut down North Avenue, that will save you a

couple minutes. The warehouse he's taking you to is on the east side of town. There was a fire in it last year, and it hasn't been rebuilt yet. You can make it."

She focused on Kendrick's voice in her ear. "I'm scared."

She'd never admitted that to anyone in her adult life.

"It's okay to be scared. Scared doesn't mean you can't handle it. We're on our way. And Gabe's jet has landed in Denver. We just need a little more time."

"I'm afraid to stall him. I'm afraid he'll hurt Maggie."

"Don't stall. Give him what he wants."

"Survive now, figure out the rest later," she murmured.

"Exactly."

It got quiet and fear squeezed her heart. Had he disconnected. "Kendrick?"

"I'm here."

"I . . ." She faded off. She didn't really have anything to say.

"I'm not going to leave you. I'm going to be right here the whole time. Right with you."

"Thank you." Her throat was tight around the words.

"No need to thank me. There's nowhere else in the world I would rather be. A chance to be inside your head when you can't get rid of me? Dream come true."

She smiled. Kendrick was the only person on the planet who could get her to smile in a situation like this.

But her smile faded as she pulled up to the warehouse and her phone rang again. She grabbed it. This call wasn't from Varela and when she hit receive, a video started playing. A live feed of Porter outside of Maggie's house, in her backyard, walking toward a sliding glass door, knife in his hand. Maggie was sitting with her mom at the kitchen table. It looked like they were doing homework or something.

The video cut off.

She couldn't stop the sobs that escaped her. "Oh God."

"Neo, what happened?" Kendrick asked.

"He's there. Video. At the house. He's there." She grabbed her phone, the computer, and the drive and bolted for the warehouse door.

"Gabe is closing in, and we're right behind you. Stay strong, baby."

She didn't respond to Kendrick. Her only thought was to let Varela know she'd arrived. She slammed through the warehouse door that had been left cracked open. "I'm here, you bastard. Call Porter off!"

Varela stepped out from the shadows. "Seems like you can work more quickly when you're properly motivated."

"Fuck off." She was breathing much heavier than she should've been from the short run from the car, but she couldn't get her heart to stop pounding. "Stop Porter right now, or I swear to God I will destroy this drive, and you will lose everything."

Varela raised an eyebrow at her, but he brought his phone up to his ear. "Stand down." His eyes never left Neo's. "But if you don't hear from me every five minutes, then resume immediately. Make it messy and painful."

It took every ounce of willpower she had not to double over and vomit.

"All right, Neo, it looks like you've got five minutes to show me what your daughter's life is worth."

Chapter 28

Having Neo in that warehouse alone with that bastard, knowing he was the one who'd had her beaten so badly, had Kendrick twitching with the need to do violence himself.

"She's barely holding it together," he murmured to Ian. They were in his vehicle, racing toward the warehouse.

"She's tough. She'll make it through."

Kendrick didn't doubt that. Neo could handle whatever she had to. He just wished she didn't have to handle so damned much.

He was in the car with Ian and Gavin. Zac and Finn were following them in Finn's Jeep. The others had stayed behind to make sure the kids were safe.

They were five minutes behind Neo. Five minutes they'd used to grab enough weaponry and equipment from the Linear storehouse to launch a haphazard offensive. Kendrick was glad they had it, but he didn't want to think about what could happen in five minutes when Neo was at Varela's mercy.

"You know Varela isn't in that warehouse alone," Gavin said. Ian had Finn and Zac on his vehicle's speakerphone.

"And that place is going to be nearly impossible to sneak up on. They have all line-of-sight advantages."

"We've got thermal sensors," Zac responded. "So we'll at least have some intel before we make our move."

Kendrick pressed Dorian's comm device deeper into his ear so he could hear Neo's conversation in the warehouse.

"You called at the worst possible moment, Varela," she said. "I had just tried something new with the drive and was about to attempt a download and get real access when you decided to up your timetable. So now I have to start over and hope for the best."

"It better not take much more than four minutes and thirty seconds."

"Do it," Kendrick said to her. "Download the drive for him. Even if we lose every bit of that data, you still do it."

He knew she couldn't respond but prayed she was listening to him. She better not do anything stupidly heroic.

He could hear her pointing out the different files to Varela as they downloaded. Good.

"Seems impressive," Varela said, obviously much closer to Neo now. "How were you able to finally crack the drive?"

She didn't miss a beat. "Blend of asymmetric cryptography and a zero-day threat. Figured out Sevier was from Ukraine and might be using letters not in the English alphabet."

"Clever girl," Varela said.

Much cleverer than Varela thought, since neither a zero-day threat nor asymmetric cryptography had anything to do with how they'd accessed the drive. Just enough hacker lingo to make Varela think he was privy to private info while hiding the truth about Sevier and the kids completely.

"How is she doing?" Ian asked.

He pressed the button so Neo wouldn't hear him. "She's holding her own."

They pulled up at a gas station a half mile away. It was the closest place they knew they wouldn't be spotted.

Finn got out of his Jeep and belly crawled closer to the warehouse so he could get the thermal imaging data they needed. If luck was on their side, it would show the building only had Neo and Varela in it.

But somehow, Kendrick didn't think Varela was that stupid.

Every instinct Kendrick had urged him to rush the building right now and eliminate the threat to Neo. Listening to her try to placate Varela—to beg every few minutes for Maggie's life—didn't ease that feeling.

It wasn't going to take long for Varela to realize Neo had done everything he needed her to do. The drive would continue to download without her. Then what use would she be to him?

Zac handed out weapons to everyone. Kendrick took both handed to him and began pacing in front of the car. "We need to move in *now*. That bastard doesn't have any reason to keep Neo alive much longer."

Zac fastened a weapon to a chest holster, then squeezed Kendrick on the shoulder. "Hang in there, Blaze. It's hard. But going in blind puts her more at risk."

Finn was back a couple minutes later, filthy from belly crawling so far. "There's five inside the building. Two relatively close together, so I assume that's Neo and Varela. The other three are positioned by upper windows and have good line of sight. It's going to be hard to get in there with them unaware."

Kendrick slammed his hand down on the hood of the car. "Then we give up the element of surprise. I'm not leaving her in there alone. I promised her we'd be coming to help."

All four men stood around him nodding but not quite agreeing yet. They were there to speak logic, develop a plan.

How many times had he been one of those nodders— calm and collected? He'd always been a watcher as one of the big, former Special Forces guys nearly lost their shit needing to help the woman they loved.

Kendrick had sympathized, wanted to do whatever he could to help, but he'd never truly understood. Not even close. Not like he did now.

The burn of terror's blade slicing him in a thousand tiny cuts with each breath of knowing he was too far away to help. The feeling of time disappearing with each unrecoverable second.

The knowledge that the world out here wasn't worth living in if the woman in there didn't survive to live it with him.

"I'm going in."

"Blaze—"

"Kendrick—"

"Goddammit—"

He held up a hand to stop everyone. "I'm going in, and I'll provide you a distraction. I'll get Varela's men over near him. The rest is up to you guys."

Ian handed him the car keys, shaking his head. "I hope this doesn't get you killed, brother."

Kendrick handed him the earpiece. At least they'd be able to communicate with Neo. "I'd rather get killed in there with her than sit out here wondering if there was something I could've done."

Ian clapped him on the shoulder. "Buy us as much time as you can."

He jumped behind the wheel and started the car, driving recklessly that last half mile, pulling up a few feet in front of the warehouse door.

"I'm coming in, Neo. Work with me, baby," he muttered. He didn't have the comm device, so saying the words didn't help. He hoped she would understand what he was about to do and play along.

"You little bitch!" He ran into the warehouse, screaming. "I can't believe I trusted you twice."

Kendrick pulled out one of the guns Zac had given him and pointed it at the drive. "There's no way I'm going to let you guys have that information."

He pointed a second gun directly at Varela's head, where he stood to the side. Kendrick could see one of the other three men but still needed to draw out the other two.

"Tell your guy to back off, Varela. He may shoot me, but I'm going to get you and that drive on my way down. I promise you that."

And he meant every last word.

Varela held up a hand. "Stand down, don't shoot Kendrick . . . yet." He turned to Neo. "But if Porter doesn't hear from me in three minutes for our next update, you know what's going to happen, Neo. Every five minutes."

Neo stepped in front of the drive. "I'm sorry I used you, Kendrick, but I can't let you destroy the drive. There's too much at stake."

She'd already figured out what Kendrick was doing and was playing along.

"I don't care what's at stake," he sneered. "I don't care how much he's paying you. It can't be worth it."

"You don't know anything about me."

Even knowing they were both acting, those words out of her mouth hurt him.

In a different reality, this was how it would've gone down if she hadn't trusted them. She would've been in this all alone, trying to manage everything without any support.

Or she would've killed herself. *Taken herself out of the equa-*

tion—as if those words made the idea any more acceptable. She'd valued everyone's life more highly than her own. Varela wouldn't have seen that coming, and it would've been an effective play. Maybe her only available play to stop him.

But it wasn't her only play anymore. She had an entire family that had her back now. Varela hadn't seen that coming either.

"Oh believe me, Neoma. I know *everything* I need to know about you."

He said it with a sneer, but the words were still true. He did know everything he needed to know about her, enough to know he was in love with her and had been for a long time.

And damn it, he still needed to take her on that first date.

It was time to kick this up a notch. The sooner it was over, the sooner her could get Neo safely out of here.

He shot one of his guns up into the air, hoping it would draw the other two men away from their lookouts.

"How could you fucking do this?" he screamed at Neo. "Get out of the way! I don't want to hurt you, but I will."

"Mr. Varela, I have a clean shot." A second voice spoke from the corner. Okay, he had two of Varela's three men focused on him. That was the best he was going to be able to do. He hoped it was enough for the guys to breach the building.

He hoped he wasn't about to get shot in the head. He didn't need degrees from Harvard and Yale to realize that the chances of this going off without a hitch were slim at best. The timing would have to be perfect.

All he could do now was trust in the abilities of the people he'd come to call family.

Neo's eyes were panicked. She was even more aware of how precarious their situation was.

"Your guy shoots me and I'll die, but you'll lose everything," he reminded Varela, praying it would be enough.

"You shouldn't have come here, Kendrick," Neo said, voice distraught. That wasn't acting. "You didn't have to be involved in this at all."

They were running out of time. They both knew it.

"What is he paying you?" he asked Neo, his eyes willing her to be strong. "Whatever it is, you know Ian DeRose can pay more. It's not too late."

"I'm fairly certain Neo is not going to quit working for me." Varela's voice fairly dripped with smugness. "What I'm paying her, even DeRose can't match. I'm quite sure of it. And I'm fairly certain you're not going to shoot Neo or the drive."

Come on, guys. It's now or never. They were out of time.

Kendrick felt his phone buzz in his pocket but couldn't lower either weapon to see what the message was.

But as soon as Neo's eyes widened, he *knew*. He'd seen her nearly every day for the past year and never once had he seen such a look of relief—of utter *peace*—come over her. She'd just gotten word in her earpiece.

Maggie and her family were safe.

"It's over," she said, voice choked with emotion. "The team has them. Ian says stay alive for eight more seconds."

He smiled at her. "That's good, because these guns are getting heavy."

"What the fuck are you two so happy about?" Varela screeched.

Neo ignored him and took a step toward Kendrick. "But you look very sexy. All *Matrix* and shit. Just need a trench coat."

He winked at her. "Who's Neo now, baby?"

Two seconds later, Varela's men fell all around him, the two Kendrick could see and a third confirmed by a groan and thump farther in the shadows. Kendrick didn't know if the guys had used bullets, tranquilizers, or some sort of Vulcan nerve pinch to take out Varela's men, and he honestly didn't care. He lowered his guns.

"You lose, asshole." Neo walked over to stand in front of Varela.

Kendrick knew what was coming, but there was no way in hell he was going to stop her. He only wished he had a camera.

Her right hook to the jaw sent Varela flying back onto his ass. She followed it up with a kick to the ribs that had the man moaning in pain. Good. She should give him another dozen to level the playing field.

"Your daughter and her family are going to die horribly," he gasped out.

Kendrick got his phone out of his pocket. Sure enough, there was the image of Gabe and Aiden with Porter in custody.

"Nobody's dying today at your hand." He tossed the phone to Neo.

She smiled, then spun it so Varela could see it. "You have no more leverage over me."

"What?" Varela sputtered, face a mottled red. "How?"

"Because she's not in this alone, you bastard." Kendrick wanted to kick the man again himself.

The Linear guys and Ian walked in, dragging Varela's men behind them. Their hands were secured behind their backs, so evidently they were only unconscious, more's the pity.

"Neo has a family," Zac said. "And this family doesn't take it lightly when one of our own is threatened."

Ian walked over and crouched in front of Varela. "And you're about to become part of *my* family. You're going to work for me to help take your bosses down, or I'm going to make sure you're thrown into a dark cell that'll eventually become your grave."

For the first time, Kendrick understood the term deafening silence.

"You can't do that," Varela finally sputtered. "I have rights."

Ian's face was cold, without an ounce of sympathy. "I'm not the law. I'm just the one who's going to make sure Mosaic goes down and stays down this time." He pulled Varela's arms behind his back to restrain him.

Kendrick walked over to Neo and tucked a strand of newly brown hair behind her ear.

"Want to get one more kick in?" he whispered in her ear as Ian dragged Varela to his feet.

"I think Ian's going to do all the kicking—metaphorically and maybe actually physically. I've gotten my justice."

"Ian is a little fucking scary."

Neo looked at him, eyes wide. "I know."

"You two know I can hear you, right?" Ian asked, grinning at them over his shoulder.

But even his smile was sharp. This was a man on a mission to take down Mosaic. Kendrick and Neo would help him whatever way they could.

Kendrick grabbed Neo's hand and led her toward the door. "I would like to take you on that date we've been talking about."

She wrapped her arms around his waist and pulled him close. "I'd like that too. And I know exactly where I'd like to take you."

He tilted her chin up with his thumb so he could kiss her. He planned to spend the next couple of decades kissing her.

"Oh yeah? Where's that?" he asked against her lips.

"Denver."

Chapter 29

"Have you ever gone up to the door? Ever wanted to meet Maggie face-to-face?"

Kendrick had never expected to spend his first date with Neo sitting in a parked car down the street from a rather unremarkable house in the suburbs of Denver. But then again, when had anything he'd ever done with Neo been normal?

He would take this over a fancy restaurant any day. Learning about the person she'd been as a child and teenager, the dreams she'd had, the life she'd led, the choices she'd made . . . and how they'd made her into the woman he loved.

A romantic dinner didn't hold a candle to truly under-standing someone. That was true romance.

"No. That's Maggie's family. I would never want to encroach on that. She's happy, well-adjusted . . . That's enough."

"Is it hard for you? Was it hard to give her up?"

Neo leaned back in the driver's seat. "I was sixteen years

old. I was making bad decisions like it was my full-time job—hence getting knocked up without even knowing who the father was. I'd just been sent back to the group home from yet another foster family who felt like I was a bad influence on their other kids because I sat in front of the computer as many minutes in a day as I could get."

If only someone had tried to understand her then. "Did it ever occur to anyone in your life that a computer was where your talents lay? To encourage you in your computer skills?"

She gave him a half smile. "If you think I'm not very warm and fuzzy now, you should've seen me then. I was one crisis after another."

"Sounds like normal teenager stuff to me."

There was no telling where Kendrick might've ended up if he hadn't had his parents to provide him with opportunities to focus and learn. More importantly, they'd provided boundaries for him. Someone for him to butt up against to test his own intellect, his skills, his will. All within the framework of knowing that they loved and accepted him no matter what.

Neo had never had anything even close to that.

"In some ways, getting pregnant was the best thing that ever happened to me. It forced a lot of changes in my life. It was the first time I seriously hacked into a system. I changed all my data so that the foster system and hospital thought I was eighteen, no longer a ward of the state and completely on my own. Then I started looking into adoption. I was at least smart enough to know there was no way I could raise a baby on my own."

"Understandable."

"Trust me when I say that no one has ever been more thoroughly vetted than Raphael and Joyce Aquino. I probably know more about them, their medical and financial histories, and their pasts than they know about themselves."

He smoothed a hand down her hair. "It was your way of protecting Maggie. You used what you had to make the best of tricky circumstances. You did it then and were still doing it with the whole Varela situation."

They both watched as Maggie sat out on the front porch with a girlfriend. They were both laughing, one of them jumping up to do some sort of crazy dance every few seconds.

Joyce had stuck her head out the door a few minutes ago and asked the girls something. Whatever they'd responded had made her laugh and roll her eyes. The way the mother of a preteen should.

"I put measures in place so that when she turns eighteen, if she decides she wants to find me through one of those DNA-testing kits or any of the adoption matching websites, I will be notified. But for right now, she has parents, friends, a wonderful life. That's the most I could ever have dreamed of. I hope she doesn't hate me."

"She doesn't. Look at that kid." Maggie had jumped up to do the dance again. "She doesn't have a bit of hate inside her. She will understand that you made an unselfish choice that was extremely difficult. You protected her."

"Do you really think she'll see it that way?"

He trailed a finger down her cheek. "I do. Because she's partially you, and that means she's at least half brilliant."

"I hope so. If she never feels the need to reach out to me, I'm okay with that because it means she's never felt like she has holes she needs filled. But if she does, I want to be able to say that everything I did for her I did out of love."

He took her hand. "There's no doubt that is true."

"I worried a little, you know, when I first placed her for adoption. How could parents truly love a child that wasn't their own? That's always been a nagging doubt in the back of my mind, and I think it's why I came here every year on Maggie's birthday. To make sure she was still just as loved."

"That's totally understandable."

"But talking to Dorian and Ray? Seeing them with Theo and Savannah?" She shook her head in wonder. "Do you remember what Dorian said?"

Kendrick did remember. " 'These are our kids. They're ours.' "

"Just like that," she whispered. "It made me realize that Raphael and Joyce love Maggie just as fiercely. Biological ties are not the most important when it comes to family."

"No, they're not."

She blew out a breath and looked at him. "Thank you for making sure she was safe even when I couldn't. I hate to think that I would've given up that drive to Varela, but the truth is I would have. I'm sorry."

He scooped her up and pulled her into his lap, both of them wincing from their injuries but neither caring. "She's your daughter. You never have to apologize for keeping family safe. I will always do whatever it takes to keep her safe also."

"She may not really be mine, but I wanted to share her with you. I wanted you to know everything. I don't want to keep secrets from you anymore."

"Since we're sharing secrets, I guess I should share mine also."

"Okay." Her voice was a little shaky.

"I've been half in love with you from the moment you showed up in Oak Creek."

A beat. "And . . . ?"

"And nothing." He pulled back so he could see her face. "Is that not enough of a secret for you?"

"I thought maybe the past few days might have changed that."

He tucked her against his shoulder. "No. If anything, the opposite. You were willing to die for someone you love. You couldn't be any more amazing."

"I'm not good at romance, Blaze. Not good with mushy words. I'm too analytical. Too practical."

"Too smart-assy."

"Yeah, maybe." There was a small smile in her voice. She pulled back so she could see him this time. "But I would die for you also. To protect you, to keep you safe. Anything that was in my power, I would give."

He understood what she was trying to say. That the words didn't come as easily to her as they did him. But he'd had a lifetime of people telling him they loved him.

She'd get a lifetime of hearing it too. From him. From his parents when he took her to meet them, which would be as soon as possible. She was going to get tired of hearing how loved she was.

Her words would come. He could wait.

He leaned forward and kissed her. "I love you too, New Moon. You know that's what Neoma means, right? The first lunar phase. Symbolizes new beginnings."

"New beginnings," she repeated, leaning her forehead against his. "I'll take it. As long as I'm starting with you."

"Damn straight you will."

They watched as Maggie and her friend jumped up, did their crazy dance, then ran inside.

"Thank you for coming here with me."

"I wouldn't have missed it. Now how about if we go on a real first date?"

"I would be honored, Mr. Foster. If you'll run me by a store so I can buy a dress first."

"Deal. Our date, and then it's time to get back and fight

the good fight. We've got work to do. Kids' identities to build, a criminal organization to shut down."

She smiled as she climbed back over to her side of the car. "I guess I'm officially part of the Linear Tactical team now."

"No. You're officially part of the Linear Tactical *family*."

Epilogue

Ian DeRose – 2 months later

I'D NEVER UNDERSTOOD the concept of small town charm until I'd come to Oak Creek, Wyoming.

Granted, I was taking a lot of shit from the Zodiac team for how much time I'd been spending here the past couple of months. I'd been able to play it off as my determination to take down Mosaic.

And that was nothing less than the truth. I *would* fucking take down Mosaic.

But Zodiac Tactical was one of the best security contracting firms for a reason, and my real purpose for being in Oak Creek wasn't fooling anyone. If it had, I'd probably have to fire them.

I parked in front of the tiny, two-room office building I'd rented for when I was here doing business. As I got out, my hand slipped into my pants pocket and pulled out the small piece of paper.

I had literally dozens of these. They were all over my

office and penthouse in Denver. Tiny paintings, about the size of a sticky note, all given to me by the woman I hadn't been able to get out of my mind since the moment she'd nearly given me a concussion with that tray of hers.

The hand-size paintings were always intriguing. Bursts of colors, creative, and full of life, like the woman herself.

Wavy Bollinger.

I definitely had not been expecting her. I wasn't someone who was caught off guard easily, but everything about this woman had caught me off guard, and kept me coming back here to Oak Creek.

Knowing I was going to see her today, after what had happened between us last time, had me rushing into my makeshift office. The sooner I got finished with my work here, the sooner I could go see her.

On the back of the tiny painting, in her delicate, flowery script, she'd said she had a surprise for me. There weren't many people in the world who could surprise me, but I had no doubt she was one of them.

Because I had no idea what she was thinking when she said *surprise*. Could be a new type of pie at the Frontier Diner. Or a waterfall off one of the nearby trails that she wanted to show me.

Or it could be her naked in my bed with a pair of hand-cuffs to be put to creative use.

There was just no telling, and thus . . . here I was in Oak Creek once again.

Eventually, she and I were going to have to talk about that. Now that Varela was dead and no longer spying on Mosaic for me, there wasn't much official reason for me to come here.

Maybe I could talk Wavy into living near one of the Zodiac Tactical offices—there were quite a few to choose from. She'd mentioned being ready to get out of Oak Creek, and if she picked somewhere near a Zodiac office, I'd be moving headquarters there.

Or if she wanted to live somewhere else, it looked like I'd be opening a new Zodiac Tactical office. The thought brought a smile to my face. Smiling . . . something I'd been doing more and more of. It didn't even feel awkward anymore.

And who was to blame for that?

The package sitting at my front office door had me pulling out the weapon I always carried in a shoulder harness.

There should be no mail here. All mail was rerouted into town or to one of my other offices. I stepped closer. My name was written on the outside of the box and nothing else. Definitely suspicious.

Taking a step back, I got Landon on the line, placing my phone on speaker mode.

"What's up, Boss? Did Wavy clock you with another tray?"

I cut him off. "I've got an unaddressed package by the front door of my building here in Oak Creek."

Landon immediately turned serious. We both remembered what had been in the last package that had arrived for me, unaddressed, at our Denver office. Silas Varela's thumb, and a picture of his murdered body.

"Run the scanner and the cameras here. See if you can get any info on who left this thing."

"Roger that. I'm running it now," Landon said. "Give me a few minutes. And for God's sake, don't touch that box."

Being out here in a relatively unsecure location wasn't the smartest way for me to run my business, so we'd put high-security measures in place. Cameras everywhere and infrared sensors to be able to tell remotely if someone was

JANIE CROUCH

inside the building. I could've checked it from my phone, but I'd rather keep my weapon out and let Landon do it.

Because there should be no box here. No one outside the company should've known about this place at all.

As soon as Landon assured me the building was clear, I would grab the technology that would allow me to make sure there was no explosive inside.

"Boss, we've got a problem," Landon told me. "Building is clear, but the cameras were switched off manually a few days ago. I'll have to check into that further."

Fuck. There was no reason for him to check further. *I* was the one who'd taken the cameras offline last week because of what I'd been doing with Wavy. There was no way in hell I'd risk anyone else seeing her like that.

"No need, Landon. I took the cameras offline and forgot to put them back on." Because I'd pretty much forgotten my own name by the time Wavy had been done with me. "Reconnect them now and get them running."

I still kept my weapon out as I went inside, but there was no indication anyone had been here. I knew Landon would already be sending a backup team and they would check more thoroughly when they got here.

I scanned the package with our equipment. It was clear, so I grabbed some latex gloves out of a crime kit in the back room.

"Okay, we're not working with explosives," I said. "I'm going to open it."

"Ian, you need to wait until a backup team gets there."

"No." My gut was screaming that there was something really wrong. "I need to find out what this is all about."

"Fine." Landon let out a sigh, his fingers clicking on a keyboard. "But I'm at least calling some of the Linear guys to come over as backup. This feels ugly."

It did feel ugly.

I crouched down in front of the box about twice the size of a shoe box. I slid on a pair of latex gloves and used my pocket knife to cut through the tape.

Inside the box was another smaller box. Great. Someone wanted to play games. I switched the call to video and propped up the phone so Landon could have a closer view of what I was doing.

I opened the second box only to find a third, smaller one inside.

"Okay," I said, "Someone is fucking with us. This is a Russian nesting doll in box form."

There were seven boxes in all. Inside the last box was a square envelope with writing on the outside.

What price are you willing to pay to win this war?

"Whatever price I have to, asshole," I muttered as I turned the envelope to open it.

"Ian, wait. I don't like this," Landon said, but I didn't stop.

I needed to know.

Whatever game Mosaic was playing with me now, I was ready, because I was going to win. They were going down. I didn't have Varela anymore, but I'd find another way.

I eased open the envelope with the knife. The first thing I saw was a photo of Wavy, smiling in a red polka dot dress. It almost brought a smile to my own face until I saw what she was doing, who she was smiling at.

She was shaking the hand of Erick Huen, one of the highest-ranking members of Mosaic that we'd successfully identified. She was standing next to him, smiling at him, shaking his hand.

I stood and ran for my car.

"Jesus," Landon said. "Was that Wavy with Erick Huen?"

"Yes." I peeled out of the driveway and headed into town.

I didn't know what the photo meant. Was Huen threatening her? Trying to let me know he could get to her? How long ago had the photo been taken? I'd just talked to Wavy this morning, and we were supposed to meet a little later this afternoon once she got off her shift at the diner.

I had to see Wavy for myself.

"Landon, we need to figure out why she was with Huen. She needs to know what a danger he is." I hung up and slammed my foot on the gas.

Erick Huen had been around her. The thought made me absolutely sick. He was one of the worst of the Mosaic members. One of the cruelest, one of the ones I was most eager to take down.

I pulled up at the Frontier Diner a few moments later and ran inside.

"Hey there, honey." Leeann, the older waitress who worked with Wavy, smiled at me. "What are you doing here?"

"Where's Wavy?" I demanded, unable to even be civil until I saw her with my own eyes.

"She's not here. Oh, that's right, she didn't tell you. She wanted it to be a surprise."

My heart hammered against my ribs. She wasn't here. Something about her surprise.

"She's gone into Reddington City to meet with that art dealer," Leeann continued. "Some agent who was interested in her work and wanted to meet her for lunch."

Fear closed around my throat. "Where? When?"

"Here's the card he gave her yesterday when he came in the diner looking for her." Leeann grabbed a business card sitting by the register and handed it to me.

Louis Noeya, art agent.

But the picture was Erick Huen.

"Wavy was all excited. Had her red polka dot dress on. Her lucky dress, she calls it." Leeann winked at me. "She said she hoped to get lucky twice today, if you know what I mean."

I couldn't breathe. I couldn't even say anything to Leeann. I turned and ran back outside, the business card in my hand.

My phone rang again, and I answered, knowing it was Landon.

"They have her," I whispered, unable to say anything else. "Mosaic has Wavy."

I looked at the business card again, the letters that made up the name, Louis Noeya, morphing as the anagram became clear.

Louis Noeya spelled *You lose Ian*.

Mosaic had Wavy.

*****

Thank you for reading BLAZE! Wavy and Ian's compelling story continues in CODE NAME: ARIES.

Acknowledgments

A special thanks to my alpha/beta readers, editors and proofers of BLAZE (and all the Linear Tactical books): Marci, Susan, Dee, Marilize, Tesh, Diana, Aimee, Karen, Lynda, Mary, Sharon, Sammye, and Elizabeth at Razor Sharp Editing. I appreciate your dedication and keen eyes. Thank you!

And I say it all the time, but it bears repeating... a huge thanks to Deranged Doctor Designs who not only created the cover for BLAZE, but crafted ALL the Linear Tactical covers. I am always so proud to show off my books and you're the geniuses behind making them look so good.

Writing BLAZE was bittersweet. For thirteen books, the Linear characters have been like family to me. It's hard for me to walk away from Oak Creek, but it's time. Maybe someday I'll be back.

But now we move on. I hope you'll take the leap with me into the Zodiac Tactical world. As you can see from the epilogue here, that series is going to be an adventure. (And I'm so excited!!)

Yes, it will be different. Different characters, different

locations, different perspectives. I'm changing and growing and trying new things as an author to keep my work fresh. The Zodiac Tactical series is allowing me to do that.

But the stuff that matters—the chemistry, the action, the community that becomes a family—those elements will *always* be in my books.

I can't wait to bring you Ian and Wavy's full story.

Thank you, my reader friend, for taking this journey with me. It has been my honor and privilege to write the Linear Tactical books.

Believe in heroes,
Janie

Also by Janie Crouch

ZODIAC TACTICAL RESCUE UNIT
Code Name: ARIES

LINEAR TACTICAL SERIES (series complete)
Cyclone

Eagle

Shamrock

Angel

Ghost

Shadow

Echo

Phoenix

Baby

Storm

Redwood

Scout

Blaze

Forever

INSTINCT SERIES (series complete)
Primal Instinct

Critical Instinct

Survival Instinct

About the Author

"Passion that leaps right off the page." - Romantic Times Book Reviews

USA Today and Publishers Weekly bestselling author Janie Crouch writes what she loves to read: passionate romantic suspense featuring protective heroes. Her books have won multiple awards, including the National Readers Choice and Booksellers' Best.

After a six-year stint in Germany (due to her husband's job as support for the U.S. Military) Janie is back on U.S. soil and loves hanging out with her four teenagers. Sometimes.

When she's not listening to the voices in her head—and even when she is—she enjoys engaging in all sorts of crazy adventures (200-mile relay races; Ironman Triathlons, treks to Mt. Everest Base Camp) traveling, and trying new recipes.

Her favorite quote: "Life is a daring adventure or nothing." ~ Helen Keller.

facebook.com/janiecrouch

amazon.com/author/janiecrouch

instagram.com/janiecrouch

bookbub.com/authors/janie-crouch